Adelaide is stunned when Josiah proposes marriage.

Her thoughts swirled in a flurry of confusion. He wanted her to marry him? She gulped. Before she could utter a word, he continued.

"Please understand. I acknowledge it's a marriage of convenience. We would marry in name only. I would respect and honor you. You would cook for the crew. In return, you would experience life on the sea." He searched her eyes, as if trying to read her answer. "It's the only proper way for you to sail."

Mixed emotions closed in, making it difficult for her to breathe. How long had she dreamed for this day? Yet marriage? She hadn't thought of that. Marriage was saved for love, wasn't it? Still, why hadn't she seen this coming? He and Mrs. Markle were right. Adelaide couldn't possibly sail the seas as a single woman. What foolishness that she had allowed her dreams to carry her onto a ship without thought of propriety.

Well, Josiah was her friend, after all, not a total stranger. His love had died with his first wife, so there would be no romantic illusions on Adelaide's part. A business deal. How odd that she should feel a tug of sadness.

"I know this is all so sudden, but—"

"I'll go." Her dreams would come true—or did she seal a fate of loneliness and endless days without knowing love?

DIANN HUNT resides in Indiana with her husband. They have two grown children and two grandchildren. Feeling God has called her to the ministry of writing, Diann shares stories of lives changed and strengthened by faith in a loving God.

Books by Diann Hunt

HEARTSONG PRESENTS
HP 507—Trunk of Surprises

A Whale of a Marriage

Diann Hunt

Heartsong Presents

A note from the Author:
I love to hear from my readers! You may correspond with me
by writing:

> **Diann Hunt**
> **Author Relations**
> **PO Box 719**
> **Uhrichsville, OH 44683**

ISBN 1-59310-070-1

A WHALE OF A MARRIAGE

Our mission is to publish and distribute inspirational products offering
exceptional value and biblical encouragement to the masses

All Scripture quotations are taken from the King James Version of the
Bible.

All of the characters and events in this book are fictitious. Any resemblance to actual persons, living or dead, or to actual events is purely
coincidental.

PRINTED IN THE U.S.A.

one

"Mrs. Markle, times have changed. This is 1856, and women are allowed aboard whaling ships these days." Adelaide Sanborn stuffed another bolt of material into the slot on the shelf. The playful banter amused Adelaide, though she knew all the while she wasted her breath on her dear friend.

"Adelaide, I know all about the changing times. Some women are sailing, true; but mind you, those few are married women. A whaling ship is no place for a single woman, and that's the truth of it." The boards beneath Ida Markle creaked in protest as she pushed her broom in short, determined strokes.

Just then a bell jangled atop the door of the only general store in Yorksville, Massachusetts. A customer stepped inside.

A salty gust of October wind swished through the room, causing the invoices on the counter to flutter. Ida's husband, Caleb, quickly gathered the restless papers and placed them under a large scoop normally used to dish out candy from the nearby jar.

Paying no heed to the interruption, Ida continued. "Things are what they are; you can't change them. And further, if you want my advice, Adelaide, you'd better settle down and have yourself a family. Forget that fool notion of going to sea." A growing mound of sand lifted from cracks in the floor with every strong sweep of the older woman's broom.

Adelaide let out a sigh. "I don't want to have a family. Not yet. I have dreams." She stopped stocking the shelf. Lost in thought, she stared at the bolt of cloth beneath her fingers.

Ida walked over, reached up, and rested her hand on Adelaide's shoulder. "Of course it doesn't hurt to dream, dear." She paused a moment. Her voice softened. "You've worked so hard since your pa died."

Adelaide placed another bolt of cloth on the shelf and faced Ida. The older woman patted Adelaide's shoulder. "With no children to call our own, you are like a daughter to us, Adelaide. I pray you find your happiness someday." Her gaze drifted toward the window with the ocean in plain view. "Mind you, I know the dangers of the sea, and well"—she pulled a handkerchief from the pocket of her apron and wiped her nose—"I just want what's best for you, that's all."

Adelaide reached her arms around Ida's ample frame and gave her a tender squeeze. "I thank you for caring, Mrs. Markle. I'm sorry for carrying on so. You know I've always been too independent for my own good."

Mrs. Markle let out a chuckle. "That you have, dear. That you have." She patted her nose once more, then stuffed the handkerchief back into her pocket. With a swish of her broom, she continued on her way across the floor.

Once Adelaide finished stacking the various bolts of material, she gathered a pile of oil pants into her arms, then walked toward the bare shelving in the front of the store. Taking great care, she stacked the pants in organized rows.

No matter how hard she tried, Adelaide's passion for the sea overcame her good sense most times. She knew that. She also knew she could not bear the thought of living a dreary life on land.

She supposed she should give up on the notion of sea life altogether, yet something deep inside compelled her forward. A stirring. A longing she couldn't describe to anyone. After all, what woman would understand how Adelaide's heart quickened with the arrival of a long-awaited whaling ship, or how stories of the crew's adventures would fill her dreams and waking moments? Such ideas made most womenfolk squeamish.

With much regret, she resigned herself to the fact that there was little she could do about it. So each afternoon she stood outside the general store and watched the distant docks where families clustered to wave good-bye to the brave sailors. The big ships rolled out of the bay into the expanse of ocean that would be their home for months to come. Adelaide dreamed of being carried out to sea with them.

"Morning, Josiah," Caleb Markle called to the customer.

Until that precise moment, Adelaide hadn't noticed who had entered. She glanced up to see Josiah Buchanan, known around the village as the best of all whaling captains. She'd heard of his adventures at sea. Folks said year after year he brought in the biggest catches of the deep. Many times his ship carried sperm whale, the richest cargo a whaling ship could haul into port.

Adelaide went over to sort through the woolen shirts and catch a better look at him. His muscular frame towered, she guessed, slightly over six feet. She stole glances and noted his confident walk. She studied his profile. A strong, sturdy jaw suggested that most likely once he made up his mind, it would not be easily changed. She decided he had the appearance of a grand sea captain. Absently rubbing her hands along the thick wool and pushing aside all remembrances of proper etiquette, she continued to watch him.

The warmth from the potbellied stove caused her to slip into her usual daydream, the one that always carried her out to sea.

Josiah turned her way. He took off his cap. "Morning, ma'am."

Adelaide snapped to attention and muttered a short greeting. She spun around to hide the color she felt rise up her cheeks. What would he think of her, gazing at him like a silly schoolgirl! The very idea! Not that it mattered. He didn't know who she was and certainly would not care to find out.

"So you want to sail the seas, do you?" The strong voice was beside her now.

Adelaide glanced up with a start. Her breath stuck in her throat as she found herself looking into the most intense blue eyes she had ever seen. Powerful yet inviting, like the sea. She could scarcely pull herself away.

"I. . ." She got no further, for the word lodged itself midway in her throat. Adelaide swallowed hard. Suddenly it seemed of the utmost importance for her to straighten imaginary wrinkles from her dark skirt. With some effort, she pulled in a long breath. "Very much," she finally managed. She tried to speak the words lightly, but passion weighed them down.

"I told her the sea is no place for a woman. I'm sure you quite agree, isn't that right, Captain Buchanan?"

From the reflection in the storefront window, Adelaide could see Ida had joined them, hands placed firmly on her hips, clearly waiting on Captain Buchanan to echo her beliefs.

Turning to them, Adelaide looked first to Josiah for his response. Her heart paused as she waited for him to speak. It should not concern her to know his position on the matter, yet somehow it did. Before she could think further, Josiah broke the silence.

His mouth split into a wide grin. He looked at Ida. "Seems to me if I'm going to engage in so lively a debate, I ought to at least be introduced to this lovely young lady." He turned his smile toward Adelaide.

Ida pulled her hand to her mouth and covered a slight giggle. "Oh, my, of course." She cleared her throat and seemed to pause for effect. With a sweep of her hands, she began, "Josiah Buchanan, I would like to introduce you to Adelaide Sanborn. Adelaide, Josiah."

"It's my pleasure to meet you. . .Mrs. Sanborn?"

"Oh, my, no, she's not married," Ida said as she absently straightened a pile of mittens. "She's about as easy a catch as a sperm whale." Ida laughed heartily at her own comment until she spotted Adelaide's expression. The old storekeeper feigned a cough and busied herself further with the mittens.

Adelaide thought she heard Caleb chuckle across the room. She stood speechless, wishing with all her might that the sea would break through the store and carry her away at that very moment. Before she could find her voice, Josiah came to her rescue.

His eyes held a smile. "Ah, a very worthy catch, indeed." He winked at Adelaide as if they had a private joke between them, then turned back to Ida. "Sperm whales, as you know, Mrs. Markle, are the hardest to catch, but the most worthwhile."

"Yes, well—" A slight crimson crept up Ida's neck, a sure sign she was flustered. Seemingly at a loss for words, she turned to join her husband.

Feeling a bit uncomfortable with the discussion, Adelaide couldn't change the subject fast enough. "My pa served on a whaling ship."

He raised a brow. "Not Elijah Sanborn?"

"You knew him?" Excitement filled her. Five years after his death, she still found herself longing to hear of her pa's adventures.

"I knew him well. I served with him in my younger days."

Adelaide couldn't imagine how young Josiah must have been when he knew her pa. She studied him in an attempt to guess his age. *Twenty-nine, thirty, perhaps.*

"He kept the crew going with his laughter and music." Josiah's eyes took on the look of one remembering the past. He shook his head. "What a voice!"

Adelaide laughed and nodded. A comfortable pause followed. "I miss him still."

"That must be why you love the sea, because you miss him?"

"That's true, but it's more than that." A seabird swooped toward the storefront window, catching Adelaide's attention, mocking her with its freedom. "Certainly his adventurous tales livened my childhood, but I've always been different than most girls. I've wanted to go to sea for as long as I can remember. To feel the adventure of a whale hunt, to see the sunset spill upon distant waters, to watch the glimmer of moonlight as it prances across midnight waves; that's what I want." She pulled her hand to her mouth. "Oh, I'm sorry to prattle on so."

A tender smile lit his face. "Not at all. I understand completely."

She looked away but felt his gaze linger on her. Though in her mind she had imagined sea captains as stern and unbendable, she sensed this man got along well with his crew.

They both turned back to peer through the window. The sun hung in noonday position. A brisk breeze churned the ocean, causing the sun's rays to sparkle like scattered shards of glass across a base of blue. Gulls flew low over the docks. Though the store's door was closed, the afternoon air squeezed through tiny cracks, releasing a fresh, salty scent into the room.

"It is beautiful, isn't it," he commented more than asked.

"Yes. There isn't anything more beautiful." A thought struck her. Perhaps he could find a way for her to travel the seas! If he stayed around long enough, she could prove to him her longing for the sea was more than a silly notion. She might convince him to help her, maybe even convince him to take her along. . . .

"I'll be setting sail around the end of November," he said, breaking through her thoughts.

Her building dreams stretched out of reach. Not much time to convince him of her seaworthiness. "You'll be gone awhile?" she asked, trying not to show her disappointment.

"Eight to twelve months, perhaps. Maybe longer. Sometimes we don't know until we get out there just where the whales will take us."

Adelaide nodded. "I didn't mean to pry—"

He shook his head. "It's a logical question, really."

"We'll be praying for the *Courage*'s safe return," she said.

Josiah cleared his throat. "Yes, well, I thank you for that. It's nice to be remembered." He stared at her for a moment. "Maybe I'll see you at church on Sunday?"

Her heart quickened. Perhaps there was still time to gain his help. She nodded as enthusiastically as befit a proper young woman.

"Good. It was a pleasure, *Miss* Sanborn," he said, emphasizing the "Miss." With that, he turned and walked out the door, leaving Adelaide to stare after him.

The bell on the door jarred her back to reality. Looking out the window, Adelaide took a minute to calm herself. When she turned around, she found Ida Markle watching her.

"Are you all right, dear? You look a little flushed. You're not coming down with a fever, are you?"

"I'm fine. Just a little. . .tired, I suppose." Tired? How could she be tired when her heart pounded like that of a chased whale?

"No wonder, child. You've been working too hard. You didn't need to help us today. You have enough work of your own with the mending you do for people."

Adelaide nodded. "You know how I love to come here, Mrs. Markle."

Ida sighed. "To be near the sea, no doubt," she said with a tease in her voice.

"I'm fine, really."

"You let me be the judge of that. You come sit over here." Before Adelaide could protest further, Ida Markle appointed herself head nurse, promptly placing tea and crackers before the ailing patient.

The store was quiet as Ida pulled up a chair beside Adelaide. "He is quite a man, isn't he?" Ida asked with indifference as she stirred her own tea.

"Hm?"

"Mr. Buchanan. He's quite the captain, they say."

"Oh, yes. So I've heard." Adelaide sipped her tea, her thoughts tossing about like a battered ship on a restless sea.

"He was married once."

Adelaide's ears perked up.

"Catherine was her name. She kept to herself. Came into the store once in a while. Not a very friendly sort." Ida shrugged. "Before he left for the sea, she moved away. They hadn't been married long. He later got word that she died. No one ever said how she died. Must have been the plague or some such thing. Now he stays on the seas, hardly ever coming home. Folks say he loved her something fierce." Ida tapped her spoon on the rim of her cup, then took a slight swallow.

Adelaide wondered what kind of woman could capture the heart of a sea captain. Before she could come to a conclusion, her thoughts drifted back to how she might convince Josiah Buchanan to help make her dreams come true. . . .

two

Josiah dropped his other boot to the floor. What had gotten into him to tell Adelaide he would see her on Sunday? He had given up on church and friendships long ago.

There was a time when he believed the best in people, that churchgoing folks really cared, but Catherine changed all that. She used him. Took his love and threw it aside once she realized it didn't have lots of money attached to it. He had made a good living but obviously not enough according to Catherine.

If only he hadn't taken her to Yorksville, maybe things would have been different. She had grown up in Bayview, Massachusetts. Her ma still lived there, but Catherine had wanted to move to Yorksville to be near a friend. No sooner had Josiah and Catherine arrived than the friend and her husband moved out West.

Josiah paced restlessly across his bedroom, the memories battering him like a nor'easter. Catherine had delighted in the cruel words she'd flung at him when she told him she was leaving. Even as he'd chased the elusive whale, the sea's siren song failed to silence her hurtful words. She had never loved him. His eyes burned. He rubbed them as if to wipe away the memories.

The next thing he knew, he received a letter saying she had died. Before he could blink, it was over, as if it had never happened. Like the fact that she stole his heart was just a dream—or a nightmare. His fingers massaged his temples as he sat on the edge of the bed.

Josiah put on his nightclothes, climbed into bed, and stared into the darkness. In all his pain, it seemed no one had cared. At church, instead of showing compassion, folks had whispered. Some walked by without a word. Passed judgment on him, no doubt. He decided then and there that since the church folks didn't care, God must not care, either. He figured he'd just have to make it through life on his own.

Still, he couldn't deny the lonely ache in his heart. Was it for the love he lost with Catherine or something else?

❧

An unseasonably balmy sun warmed Josiah's back as he climbed from the carriage. Each step felt like he had an anchor chained to his ankle as he made his way to the church. He didn't want to be there, but being a man of his word, he had to go.

Someone called out, "Morning, Josiah."

Josiah turned to see Harrison Neal and his wife, Rebecca. "Harrison, good to see you, old man."

Harrison reached out to grab Josiah by the hand. The two men shook hands heartily.

Josiah took off his hat and turned to Rebecca. "Ma'am."

"Morning, Josiah."

"How long you here?" Harrison asked.

"Till the end of November."

"Well, it's good to have you for as long as we can." Harrison slapped Josiah good-naturedly on the back.

Josiah smiled. No matter what he thought of church and the "Christians," he always thought Harrison a good man.

"Hey, a few of the families are meeting for a picnic after church. Why don't you join us? We've plenty of food. Bring a guest if you'd like." With his elbow, Harrison ribbed Josiah in the side.

"Harrison!" Rebecca scolded.

"Aw, Becca, Josiah knows I like to tease."

Rebecca smiled and held up her head with an air of reprimand. "Just the same. . ."

"Thanks for the offer, Harrison, but I—" Josiah spotted

Adelaide. Their eyes met for an instant. Josiah turned to Harrison and saw him glance at Adelaide.

"Like I said, if you want to join us and bring a guest, you're more than welcome." Harrison laughed and pulled on Rebecca's arm. "Come on, love, it's time we get to church." He threw a wink over his shoulder at Josiah.

Though Josiah wanted to keep his distance, he didn't want to appear rude. He made his way over to Adelaide. "Good day, Miss Sanborn." His voice cracked. On his ship he spoke with authority. His mind was sharp and decisive. In front of this woman, before he could form a single word, his mind clogged with confusion and his voice crackled like a broken foghorn. Being on a ship had made him forget how to behave in front of womenfolk.

She turned to him. "Hello, Captain Buchanan."

"Beautiful day for a picnic," Josiah said as he opened the church doors for her. He couldn't imagine what made him mention the picnic. Though not interested in settling down with any woman, he had to admit the idea of a friend comforted him. Life as a sea captain could get lonely. Still, he wanted to keep his distance.

She smiled. "Yes, it is. One of the few left before winter, I'm afraid." She looked at him. "Were you about to say something?"

The words crowded just inside his mouth. Her smile shook them loose. "I don't suppose you—"

"Why, Captain Buchanan, how nice to see you," Mrs. Sanborn said with a warm smile.

"Ma'am."

"Will you be with us long, or will the sea take you away soon?"

"I'll only be around till the end of November, I'm afraid."

"Ah, I see." Mrs. Sanborn's glance went from Adelaide to Josiah and back to Adelaide. "Are you ready to sit down, Adelaide?" Before her daughter could respond, Mrs. Sanborn turned back to Josiah. "Good day, Captain." Adelaide's expression held an apology before she turned and walked away with her mother.

Josiah sat down on the bench. He appreciated Mrs. Sanborn's kindness. Still, he clearly got the feeling she didn't want him around her daughter. He wondered what people said about him. Did they blame him for Catherine's death?

ðə

Pastor Malachi Daugherty's voice boomed through the air: "Husbands, love your wives. The Bible tells us in Ephesians five, verses twenty-eight through thirty, 'So ought men to love their wives as their own bodies. He that loveth his wife loveth himself. For no man ever yet hated his own flesh; but nourisheth and cherisheth it, even as the Lord the church; for we are members of his body, of his flesh, and of his bones.'"

Josiah shifted uncomfortably on the bench as painful memories shadowed his thoughts. *Didn't I love her enough? I tried to provide for her. That's why I had to go to sea, to provide for us, for our future. The sea was the only life I knew. She didn't care; she never loved me. She wanted wealth.* Emotion crept up his throat. Someone next to him stirred, pulling Josiah to the present in time to hear the pastor's final prayer.

People slowly ambled out the church doors, talking in a friendly manner along the way.

Josiah wanted to get out of there before he ran into Adelaide again. He didn't want to give her the wrong impression.

Making his way through the tiny gathering, he offered greetings here and there until an elderly woman stopped him. She held him in conversation for a few minutes. When he turned around, he bumped into Adelaide.

"Oh, excuse me," Josiah said, turning his cap nervously in his hands.

Adelaide tossed him an understanding smile.

"Good sermon." Why did he say that? He'd hardly heard a word of it.

"Yes, it was," Adelaide agreed.

They stood in a moment of awkward silence. Josiah cleared his throat.

"So is she coming?" Josiah and Adelaide looked over and saw Harrison Neal grinning widely.

Josiah cringed. He didn't want to get himself into an uncomfortable situation before he set sail. He shot a warning glance at Harrison.

"Oh, sorry." Harrison backed away slowly and melted into the tiny crowd.

Adelaide chuckled. "What was that all about?" Her eyes teased as she waited for an answer.

Josiah sighed and stared at his cap.

"Well, are you going to tell me?"

Josiah looked up to see Adelaide smiling. Oh, what did it hurt to have a friend? He would be leaving soon, anyway. "They're having a picnic—a few of the families today. We're invited."

"We?"

"Well, Harrison asked me to come and said I could bring a guest, and, um, well. . ."

"I'd love to."

Josiah felt like he'd swallowed a fish bone. He coughed. "You would?"

"Do they have enough food?"

Could she hear his heart thumping like a hammer nailing a loose plank? "Yes, they said they have plenty."

Her eyes twinkled with amusement. "I'll let Ma know." Adelaide turned away from him, and Josiah shrugged. It wouldn't hurt to have some friendly company.

⁂

"I don't think it's proper that you should prance around the beach with Captain Buchanan, Adelaide." Ma aired her cross feelings as quietly as she could so the church people wouldn't hear.

"Ma, you know other families will be there. There's truly nothing improper about it. We will be in the open for all to see."

"That's what I'm concerned about." Ma bit her lip.

Adelaide put an arm around her ma. "I'll be fine. I will behave as a lady the entire time." Adelaide kissed Ma lightly on the forehead and felt her ma's resolve melt away.

"It's just that, well, you know how people like to talk, and I want you to be careful with your heart."

"I understand." A laugh escaped her. "It's not as though I'm getting married today, Ma."

At this, Ma couldn't help but chuckle herself. She paused for a moment. "Well, you certainly can't go without contributing something. You'll need to come home. You baked two apple pies yesterday. Take one of those."

Adelaide squeezed her mother tight. "Thank you!"

"Adelaide, watch yourself. Don't let him see you carry on so. We must keep the menfolk guessing."

"Yes, Ma."

Ma laughed behind her handkerchief.

☙

The sun sailed high in the sky, spreading its rays across the waters with flecks of gold. Josiah helped Adelaide from the carriage, grabbed the apple pie, and together they walked across the sandy beach to join the others.

The sun slipped toward the distant horizon while they passed the afternoon visiting with friends. Josiah shared stories of his whaling expeditions, and Adelaide found herself in an emotional whirlwind, caught between laughter and tears with every story. Josiah made the sea come alive to her the way her pa had done.

By the end of the picnic, Adelaide wanted to escape to the sea more than ever before. A melancholy mood shadowed her heart. She sat quietly, lost in thought.

"Have I bored you with my fish tales?"

"Oh, my, no!"

His expression relaxed. "I'm glad." They sat in silence, staring out to sea.

"Adelaide, I must say your ma's apple pie is the best I have ever eaten. You tell her I said so."

"Well, I'll be happy to tell her; however, she didn't make it." His eyebrows lifted.

"I did." She pretended a slight curtsy.

His eyes smiled in surprise. "Not only pleasing to the eye but a good cook as well!"

Not used to such compliments from gentlemen friends, Adelaide felt her face flush.

Josiah studied her for a long moment, looking as though an idea had just struck him. Before Adelaide could question him, he blurted out, "Allow me to take you to dinner tomorrow night."

Adelaide looked at him wide-eyed and hesitated.

"I'm sorry, Adelaide, I'm forgetting myself." He slapped his cap on the side of his pants like a little boy who had just been chastised.

Adelaide willed her heart to stop pounding in her ears. "Tomorrow?" She could already hear her ma's disapproval, but the idea of having more time to convince him to help her. . . "I–I—"

His eyes looked hopeful, yet something in his expression told her there was more to his request. After a moment's pause, a smile stretched across his face.

Did she dare hope? A quick flutter made her lose her breath. "Tomorrow would be just fine."

His face brightened. He pulled his cap snug on his head and gave it a jerk. "All right, then, tomorrow night at seven o'clock?"

"Why don't you come to my house? I'll cook dinner; then Ma and my sister, Esther, could get to know you better."

"If it means I get to eat more of your apple pie, I'll be there."

She smiled. "Seven o'clock, then?"

Josiah nodded. They looked around and noticed the others gathering their things and loading them onto wagons. Everyone said good-bye and headed for home. Josiah aided Adelaide into his carriage as dusk settled upon the small village. Josiah drove the carriage along the seashore; Adelaide lifted her gaze to the heavens and reveled in the stars that hung bright in the dusky sky.

With the thought of her dreams becoming a reality, Adelaide felt she would burst. "Josiah, I had a wonderful afternoon."

He coughed. "I, uh, did, too."

Could he guess her true motives? Would he mind? She suspected he had been pressured into taking her to the picnic by Harrison, but what about the dinner invitation? No doubt he spent time with her because of their common bond with her pa. She mentally shrugged. Whatever the reason, it gave her time to prove to him her love for the sea.

Once they arrived at her house, Josiah helped her from the carriage. He walked her to the door. "I'll see you tomorrow." He tipped his head, then turned and walked back to the carriage.

"Tomorrow," Adelaide whispered, her mind already wondering how she could prove herself seaworthy to this mighty captain.

three

"Adelaide Sanborn, you need to hear me out," Ma said in exasperation. She stuffed the log into the fireplace, sending the scent of pine throughout their cottage. Tiny sparks shot about, then quickly melted into the flames.

"Ma, I respect you, and I love you. But I know what I'm doing. Josiah is a gentleman. There's no harm in seeing him."

"He is a fine man, Adelaide, but you have been with him every evening this entire week. Have you lost your good sense? What will people think?"

"Ma, please, I don't care what people think! I have never fit into their mold. You know that." Adelaide felt the sting of another reminder of how different she was from other women her age. "I'm merely enjoying a friendship."

Adelaide shot a glance at Esther, who pretended not to listen as she swept the kitchen floor. "Ma, you told me I should have a gentleman caller—"

"But Captain Buchanan? He lives on a whaling ship!"

"So that's what this is about?"

"I've lived that life, Adelaide. I don't want my daughters to go through it as well!"

"He's only a friend." Adelaide hesitated a moment. She felt a lump in her throat. "Was it so terrible, Ma? Pa provided for our needs. He left us with happy memories."

The lines on Ma's face softened. "Your pa was a good man," she said quietly. Her voice grew more intense. "But that doesn't take away from the fact that I lived a very lonely life without him and practically had to raise you girls by myself. It's a hard life, Adelaide."

Silence, like a brick wall, separated them.

"Are you forbidding me to see him?"

Ma waited a moment. "No, I'm not. You are twenty-four years old, Adelaide. I had two children by the time I was your age. I'm only asking that you consider your steps wisely before taking them."

Adelaide went over to her ma and embraced her. "I will, Ma. I will."

&

Sunlight peered through the windows of the church, washing the rough benches with the light of a new day.

A family with children sat beside Adelaide. The children wiggled and scooted in their seats. Their constant movement distracted her. It took great effort for her to concentrate on the sermon.

"As you know, many of our men will be leaving within the next few weeks as the whaling ships set sail," Pastor Daugherty explained. "We hope you will join us for a farewell social this Friday, weather permitting. We've been real fortunate that the cold hasn't overtaken us just yet. Isaiah and Ethel Clemmons have graciously offered to hold the social in their barn."

After the announcement, Pastor Daugherty dismissed the congregation. People talked excitedly about the social as they left the church. Adelaide wondered if Josiah would ask her.

For all her talk of the sea, she didn't feel Josiah understood in the least what she wanted. Frustration filled her. Meeting Josiah had stirred hope to life within her. No one else she knew had the connections with ship captains that Josiah had. But he would be leaving soon, and her dreams would sail with him. Because she was a single woman, she would never experience life on the sea.

Determined to enjoy the day, she pushed aside her moodiness.

Stepping into a blaze of sunshine, Adelaide drank deeply of the damp, salty air. Nearly the end of November, it seemed a magical autumn day as the season's warmth, still refusing to give way to winter's icy breezes, surrounded them.

"Good morning, Adelaide."

Josiah's voice startled her. She felt her breath catch in her throat. "Good morning, Josiah."

People mingled all about them. The children happily ran to and fro, enjoying the moments at play while their parents talked with one another.

"If you're not tired of my company yet, I was hoping you would accompany me to the social on Friday."

Adelaide felt almost giddy with excitement. One more chance. "I would be happy to accompany you, Josiah."

Josiah nudged her elbow away from the crowd of people. "You know I'll be leaving in twelve days?"

Adelaide nodded and tried to swallow but couldn't.

He cleared his throat and kicked the ground with his boot.

"What is it, Josiah?"

He looked up at her and shook his head. "Well—"

"Adelaide, are you ready?" her ma called from behind them.

"Yes, I'll be right there," Adelaide responded over her shoulder. She looked at Josiah once more, waiting for his response.

He brushed the matter aside with a wave of his hand. "I'll talk to you about it on Friday."

Seeing he was not going to talk further, she nodded. "Friday." Secretly she was hoping she would see him before then. Every moment counted now.

"I wish it could be sooner, but I have to make preparations for sailing. Gathering my crew, loading the ship, that type of thing."

"I understand."

"Six-thirty, Friday?"

She nodded and waved good-bye. As Adelaide made her way to their buckboard, her thoughts were filled with making preparations for the social and wondering what Josiah would tell her come Friday.

❧

Josiah walked through the *Courage*, making note of inventory and wrestling with his decision. Was he taking advantage of Adelaide? Wouldn't this help them both? Over and over, he argued within himself. He stopped in front of the goose pen and checked to see what vegetables were needed. Jotting a quick note, he moved on.

Hadn't people called him "the Wise Sea Captain"? Of course, he didn't let the name go to his head. Still, he figured he had some sense of business. With heavy, dark clouds looming overhead, the skylight allowed little visibility for descending to the lower deck. Josiah stepped carefully down the steps to check on the livestock.

It seemed to him no matter how he worked the matter through, this decision seemed the best option for everyone involved. For Adelaide, for him, and for the ship. She'd certainly made it clear to him she wanted to sail. What was the harm in asking? She could always say no.

After throwing scraps to the pigs and sheep and chicken feed to the hens, Josiah trudged his way back to the upper deck. Adelaide's comments had made it obvious to him she had no idea of the harshness of sea life. That's what bothered him. He pushed aside the nagging thought that he was taking advantage of her love for the sea to meet his needs. Instead he convinced himself he was helping her live out her dream. If that helped him in the process as well, what did it hurt?

෴

Adelaide let out a contented sigh as she rode with Josiah along the seaside toward the Clemmonses' house. Although the night was a bit chilly, Adelaide thought it a perfect evening. She looked toward the glow of pink that covered the horizon with the setting of the sun. Shredded clouds floated aimlessly about. She closed her eyes and listened as the echo of the sea whispered through the evening air like a steady breeze.

"You happy?" Josiah's words broke through her contentment.

"Very." She was, too. Her hopes told her the night held endless possibilities.

"Me, too."

The distant lighthouse flashed its searching beam across the waters, threatening to shadow Adelaide's joy with thoughts of Josiah at sea and her left behind. She refused to linger there.

When they arrived at the social, Adelaide took in the scene before her. Though held in a rough barn, the place was clean and warm. Enormous trays of food lined on a large table provided plenty to eat. Local fiddlers played for the adults while children huddled in circles for stories and games.

Adelaide and Josiah passed the evening with friends and laughter. All too soon, the social drew to an end.

"Adelaide, could we go outside for a moment?" Josiah asked as he handed her some hot tea.

"Certainly." Suddenly her hopes fled and concern filled her. Was he going to say good-bye now? So soon?

They stepped into the brisk night air. Adelaide pulled her cloak closer to her neck and took a sip of tea.

Moonlight now bathed the sea in a romantic glow. The scent of homemade pies and cakes followed them from the barn, filling the air with fresh sweetness. Josiah edged her away from the barn, stepping around the front of the house facing the sea. The moon provided enough light to make their steps secure.

He turned to her. "I have something on my mind. I'm not sure how to say it."

She felt her heart turn to liquid. The next few minutes could seal her fate forever. Would her dreams come true, or would a part of her die?

"I received word my cook has decided not to sail with the *Courage.*"

Confusion filled her.

"I know you love the sea, and I thought, I mean, I was wondering, uh. . ."

Her mind tangled with his words. What was he trying to say?

He must have seen the concern on her face. He lifted his free hand. "Just hear me out before you say anything."

She nodded, trying desperately to keep her wild thoughts in check.

He looked down and nervously marked the sand with his boot. After what seemed an eternity to Adelaide, he looked out to sea as if the words he needed could be found there. "Having a good cook on my ship is one of the most important aspects of my job; the very reason I'm successful as a captain. Most ships employ a crewman, whoever they can get. I refuse to do that. The men need good food. They need their strength and health. It's a hard life out there."

He finally lifted his face to her. "What I'm trying to say is you want a life on the sea. I need a good cook for the crew. There's no time to search for one. You are a great cook."

Her heart soared! She wanted to run the beach, to shout from the rooftops, but his next words stopped her cold.

"I thought perhaps if you married me, you could have what you want, and I could as well."

Her thoughts swirled in a flurry of confusion. He wanted her to marry him? She gulped. Before she could utter a word, he continued.

"Please understand. I acknowledge it's a marriage of convenience. We would marry in name only. I would respect and honor you. You would cook for the crew. In return, you would experience life on the sea." He searched her eyes, as if trying to read her answer. "It's the only proper way for you to sail."

Mixed emotions closed in, making it difficult for her to breathe. How long had she dreamed for this day? Yet marriage? She hadn't thought of that. Marriage was saved for love, wasn't it? Still, why hadn't she seen this coming? He and Mrs. Markle were right. Adelaide couldn't possibly sail the seas as a single woman. What foolishness that she had allowed her dreams to carry her onto a ship without thought of propriety.

Well, Josiah was her friend, after all, not a total stranger. His love had died with his first wife, so there would be no romantic illusions on Adelaide's part. A business deal. How odd that she should feel a tug of sadness.

"I know this is all so sudden, but—"

"I'll go." Her dreams would come true—or did she seal a fate of loneliness and endless days without knowing love? "It is the only way I can get to the sea," she explained.

If he noticed indecision in her eyes, he said nothing. "You will? Adelaide, that's wonderful!" The thrill of the moment seemed to get the better of him. He pulled her into an enormous embrace, causing her to spill the remainder of her tea.

Oh, how she wanted to free herself from the fear of the unknown, to embrace her rescuer fully in return, to let her heart soar. Instead she bristled a little. This was not about them. This was a business arrangement. True, she would get to sail, but was this the way she wanted it?

He must have sensed her awkwardness. "Forgive me. It is such a relief to know you will go." Upon seeing her face, he cleared his throat. "Of course, we must behave as though we are happy about the whole affair in front of others, or surely they would try to stop us." His eyes searched her face.

Understanding dawned on her. That was the reason for the endless evenings together. Josiah had been working up to this point. He wanted the town to think they were courting. It all made sense to her now. "I understand, Josiah." She dropped her voice to a whisper. *What is wrong with me? This is exactly what I've wanted all my life.* Yet she couldn't stop the disappointment swelling inside. She would never have a family, never know love.

"Shall we go tell the others?"

"I'd rather you let me tell Ma alone before we make it public."

"I understand." He escorted her back toward the barn. "I

was thinking we could get married at your house in, say, five or six days?"

She turned a surprised look toward him.

"I'm sorry, Adelaide, but there isn't much time."

She nodded. The magical feel of the evening disappeared with the ebbing tide. Her life would be forever changed from this night forward. The worst fear of all grabbed her. She had not even thought to pray about the matter. . . .

&

"Oh, Adelaide, that is so romantic!" Esther said dramatically when Adelaide revealed her wedding plans.

Adelaide shifted on her bed. "Shh, I haven't told Ma yet." She could hear Ma in the kitchen. The smell of simmering vegetable soup filled their cottage.

"Oh, dear. She will not be happy about this," Esther whispered, then nervously rubbed her hands together.

"I know." Adelaide fell back against the bed. *If Ma knew the truth, she would positively forbid it.*

Esther's face brightened. "She will change her mind when she sees how happy you two are, Adelaide. She worries about us."

The room fell quiet. The only sounds came from the kitchen, where Ma clanged pots and dishes. Adelaide needed to go help. She straightened herself back up and threw a weak smile toward her sister.

"You're sure about this, Adelaide?" Esther's expression showed uncertainty.

Suddenly Adelaide knew she would have to do a better job of pretending than this. She mustered the courage and put on a happy face. "Positive."

Esther's anxious expression broke into the most pleasurable of smiles. "Don't worry, then. Everything will be fine. Now, let's go tell Ma."

Esther extended her hand to help Adelaide from the bed, and together they walked into the kitchen.

"Well, I'd wondered what you were up to. Adelaide, would

you place these bowls on the table, please? Esther, get the water."

The sisters shared a glance, then commenced to set the table. Once seated, Ma prayed over the meal, then spooned the thick soup into heavy bowls.

Esther nodded encouragement.

Adelaide took a deep breath. "Ma, I have something to tell you."

With reluctance, Ma placed the soup ladle back in the bowl and wiped her hands. As if waiting for this moment and knowing the dreaded time had arrived, Ma looked at Adelaide. "Go on."

"Josiah has asked me to marry him, and I have agreed."

"I see." Ma lifted the ladle once again and continued serving the soup.

Adelaide and Esther exchanged a glance of disbelief.

"Did you hear me, Ma?"

"I heard you, Adelaide." Ma concerned herself with the meal before them. Without looking at Adelaide she asked, "When are you leaving?" Her face remained expressionless.

"We set sail November 25. We would like to get married here, if you don't mind. Just our family with Pastor and Mrs. Daugherty and the Markles, of course."

"So your mind is made up, Adelaide?"

"Yes."

"Then there's nothing I can do to stop you." Tears glistened in her eyes as Ma turned toward Adelaide and reached for her hand. "I love you, Adelaide. I want what's best for you. I trust your judgment. If this makes you happy and you feel this is God's will for your life, I will not stop you."

Adelaide was caught off guard by her ma's response. If only Ma had scolded her, it would have made things easier. But her blessing? Her trust?

"Thank you" was all Adelaide could manage.

Plans for the wedding, which they decided would take

place in two days, consumed the rest of the mealtime.

Once alone with her thoughts that evening in bed, Adelaide felt relief that the task of telling her ma was over. The days ahead would fly by, and she mentally made a list of things she wanted to accomplish.

She knew this should be the happiest time in her life, but deceit weighed her heart. What kind of life would she have at sea? With Josiah?

"Father, what have I done?" Silent tears washed her face.

Adelaide listened as a ruffle of wind tapped against the windowpane, lightly at first, and then growing stronger. Misty rain blurred the glass. Soft thunder pealed from the heavens.

Adelaide pulled the thick blankets closer to her neck, suddenly feeling an icy chill. She closed her eyes to sleep, but the storm pulled her thoughts into a torturous theatrical play. A play in which she portrayed the lonely wife of a sea captain. . .

four

Though the wind brought fragmented conversations from nearby warehouses and other various establishments bordering the waterfront, Adelaide felt glad she had insisted the wedding take place near the *Courage*.

Just beyond their gathering, four wharves reached out more than a hundred yards into the harbor. Tethered to the wharves, eighteen to twenty whaleboats, along with dozens of smaller vessels, creaked and groaned with the churning waters that sloshed against their hulls.

The wind whipped through Adelaide's dress, causing it to snap at her feet. The noontime sun did little to warm her from the nippy breeze, but she assured herself the ceremony would be over soon and she would spend the afternoon packing before setting sail.

Josiah and his crew had spent several days loading the ship with casks of water, firewood, food, equipment, clothing, charts, medicine, nautical instruments, and the like. Adelaide could hardly believe they were almost ready to sail.

Adelaide Sanborn—rather, Buchanan—would sail on a whaling ship.

The pastor's words mingled with the murmur of the sea, and Adelaide's thoughts drifted to the evening ahead of her. Josiah had told her she would need to spend the night at his land home or people would wonder. He had assured her she could sleep in a guest room. Not that she minded. She certainly didn't want it any other way. Still, she couldn't deny it was hardly the wedding night of which a young woman dreamed.

Where were all these silly romantic notions coming from?

31

She sounded as bad as Esther. Adelaide glanced at her sister. Esther's face beamed with pure pleasure. Adelaide couldn't help but let out a slight smile.

She straightened her shoulders and turned her attention back to the pastor's words. The soft cadence of the seashore echoed against the solemn vows Adelaide and Josiah repeated in front of the few witnesses.

When they came to the ceremony's end, horror filled Adelaide as she realized Josiah would have to kiss her. Her breath felt as shallow as the shoreline. Her mind raced with the tide. She had to remain calm. Act natural. After all, this was their wedding day.

"You may kiss the bride," the pastor said with a smile.

Josiah looked uncomfortable as he reached for her, unnerving her all the more. She tried to swallow, but her mouth was too dry. *Keep up the act or the people will suspect,* she told herself. She closed her eyes, not daring to look as his face drew closer, closer. She felt his breath upon her cheeks. Still, she waited. Her heart pounded hard against her chest. It seemed an eternity. His breath grew stronger upon her skin. What was taking so long? Reluctantly, she peeked through one eye. Amusement stared back at her.

Why, he mocked her! Both of her eyes popped open. Before she could give herself over to a full fit of temper, he kissed her. Pure and simple. Just like that, taking both her temper and breath away at the same time.

It suddenly dawned on Adelaide that she had never been kissed before—unless she counted Johnny Black under the apple tree in first grade.

The tiny crowd chuckled and clapped as the couple turned to face them. Hearty congratulations filled the air, and Adelaide felt the tension fall away.

It was done.

She was now the wife of Josiah Buchanan, the grand sea captain, and Adelaide would soon sail the seas. . . .

ം

After the wedding and celebration meal, Josiah and Adelaide decided to check on the progress of the *Courage's* preparation for sea.

Stepping carefully along the wharves, they dodged barrels, boxes, cordwood, heaps of heavy chains, and various other whalecraft. Harpoons, lances, cutting spades, and oil ladles littered their path.

Adelaide watched as ship carpenters and caulkers worked to make the *Courage* sound below the waterline. She and Josiah stepped past shipwrights who busied themselves with repairing damage to the hull from previous voyages.

Once they arrived on the top deck, Josiah stopped to talk to a couple of crewmen. Adelaide looked around. She stared in disbelief at the magnitude of the square-rigged ship. Closing her eyes for a moment, she took in the sounds of the busy crew around her: the swish of the paintbrushes, the thump of hammers, men calling out to one another.

The ship stirred as heavy waves slapped against the hull. Seagulls cried overhead. Adelaide looked up to watch them swarm against the backdrop of a pure blue sky. Her eyes glanced toward the massive web of giant rope overhead. She turned portside and noticed three whaleboats slung from wooden davits and two more hung on the starboard side. Josiah had told her they would use three boats; the other two would serve as spares.

"Good afternoon, Captain," a seaman called out as he worked with others to hoist the topmast into place.

Josiah smiled and gave a quick nod.

"Is that what they call the tryworks?" Adelaide asked, nodding toward the men who worked on a brick structure forward of the fore hatch.

Josiah turned a surprised look her way. "Yes, it is. The whale blubber is cooked into oil in those large iron try-pots," he said, pointing toward the big kettles. "And the copper tank is for cooling the hot oil."

Adelaide thought it all very fascinating.

"Here's where you will spend much of your time." Josiah took her into the cookhouse.

The cookhouse. Her new job. The reason Josiah had married her. Reality seared through her romantic ideas of the sea. Adelaide glanced at the stove and goose pen where vegetables were stored. She scolded herself. After all, she couldn't sail in such a fine vessel without working like the rest of the crew. Her chin lifted. Yes, indeed, she'd pull her weight just like everyone else and be glad for the opportunity to do so. They stepped back onto the deck.

Workers nodded their greetings as she and Josiah continued on their way toward the stern of the ship. Josiah pointed out the skylight that would provide some lighting to the lower deck.

They came upon two small deckhouses connected just over the ship's helm. Adelaide caught Josiah's questioning look.

"Hurricane house, right?"

"Right again."

She noticed he seemed pleased with her knowledge of the ship. They slipped into the hurricane house, and Josiah helped Adelaide down the steps that led to the lower deck.

Painters worked hard washing the cabin and officers' quarters with a fresh coat of white paint.

Josiah stepped through the cabin and turned to grab her hand. He escorted her inside.

A couple of painters offered their greetings, then went back to work.

"This will be our room." His voice cracked.

Adelaide looked at him with a start. For a moment, his expression held a little-boy-like quality. He seemed as uncomfortable as she felt. Suddenly, the very idea made her want to giggle, but she dared not. Josiah was a proud man; she'd best not make him think she was poking fun at him.

Josiah cleared his throat.

Adelaide quickly turned and glanced around the room. The cabin held a sofa, desk, chair, and table. The adjoining room held a small washbasin and privy and a small bed hanging from gimbals. Josiah must have seen the concern on her face.

"We'll talk about that later," he whispered into her ear. His breath brushed against her face with the softness of a goose feather.

Josiah once again took her hand and led her through the lower deck, showing her the officers' cabins; the steerage rooms for the skilled workers, such as harpooners and boat-steerers; the livestock pens; and finally, in the bow of the ship, the forecastle where the foremast hands, or ordinary crewmen, slept. She looked on the room with disappointment. Thin mattresses filled sparingly with corn husks lined the bunks that would be their beds for the duration of their journey.

Josiah, seeing the concern on her face, shrugged with apology. "It's the best I can do with what the owners give me."

"I understand," she answered lightly, though concerned by the injustice of poverty and wealth.

"I guess we'd better head back so you can pack your things and move."

A smile lit her face before she could stop herself. She had to admit she could hardly wait for the new adventure awaiting her. But what did the future hold for her and Josiah? She cast a sideways glance at him and found him staring at her. He swallowed hard and turned away at once. His pace quickened, and Adelaide struggled to keep up.

She told herself to get used to it. No doubt her life would hold many challenges in the days ahead.

❧

Shoving the last bit of clothing into her trunk, Adelaide gently closed the lid and turned to find Ma and Esther standing behind her. A downcast expression covered her ma's face. Esther's eyes shone bright with dreams.

Adelaide smiled at them both. She walked over to her ma and

placed an arm around her. "I'll send letters as often as possible."

Ma nodded. She wiped the tears that stained her face. "Be happy, Addie."

Ma used Adelaide's nickname sparingly. To hear her say it nearly melted Adelaide's heart. "I am happy," Adelaide assured her. "I've always dreamed of going to sea—you know that." Seeing a flicker of surprise cross her ma's face, Adelaide quickly added, "Josiah is a good man. We'll have a wonderful life."

Ma eyed her with suspicion. Adelaide shifted from one leg to the other. Her ma knew her all too well. If Adelaide and Josiah stayed around much longer, Ma would see right through their pretense. "Well, I guess I'd better go. Don't want to keep my husband waiting." Her voice sounded much lighter than she felt.

"You're sure about this, Adelaide?" Ma's eyes studied her.

Never one to back down once she had made her choice, Adelaide answered with finality, "I'm sure." She pulled one end of the trunk; Esther quickly lifted the other. Together they carried it to the front door. Dropping it into place, Adelaide brushed her hands and looked at them once more.

"I'll miss you, Addie." Esther gave her an enormous hug.

Adelaide felt her throat constrict. "You take care of Ma," she whispered. When she pulled away, Adelaide added, "And go easy on the fellows."

Esther's eyes twinkled as her cheeks turned a rosy hue. Then a sad look crossed her face.

Adelaide knew Esther was thinking of Adam Bowman, a man who had courted her but from whom she had not heard in a while. "I'm sure you'll hear from Adam again. Don't worry," Adelaide encouraged.

Esther nodded reluctantly. "I hope you're right."

Adelaide turned to Ma. "I will miss you. You'll be all right?" Adelaide needed to hear it one more time. She had taken responsibility for the family since her pa had died, and it worried her to leave them behind. Why she worried, she didn't know. Ma and Esther were in good health, and they would do just fine without her. The enormity of her decision made her waver for a slight moment. She had allowed her passion for the sea to bring her to this point. Would it hold all the wonders of which she'd often dreamed? As much as she wanted to go, the little girl in her wanted to change her mind, run to Ma, and hide behind her skirts.

Ma took a deep breath and straightened herself. "Of course, we'll be all right," she said matter-of-factly. Her tone softened. "But we will miss you."

Ma's embrace felt like a year's worth of hugs all rolled into one. Adelaide wasn't sure if it was the tight embrace or the heavy weight on her chest that made breathing difficult.

Outside, a gentle *clip-clop* sounded the arrival of Josiah's carriage. Ma pulled away in a manner that said she didn't want to, tears still glistening in her eyes. Adelaide looked at her family. "Well, I guess I'd better go. . .to my husband."

Esther chuckled and Ma nodded.

Adelaide opened the door and looked up to see Josiah coming toward the house. "Are you ready?"

"Yes."

"Good," he said, grabbing one end of her trunk as she lifted the other. "I was hoping we could stop by the *Courage* once more to check on a matter."

Adelaide nodded.

Ma and Esther followed them to the carriage. Josiah heaved the trunk into the back.

"You'll take care of her," Ma said more as an instruction than a question.

Josiah stopped scooting the trunk and looked at Ma. "You have my word, ma'am."

Ma's shoulders relaxed. A slight smile touched her lips. "All right, then." Her practical side kicked in. "You have everything, Adelaide?"

"Yes."

Another round of hugs and tears followed, and then Josiah lifted Adelaide to the carriage. She waved good-bye to Ma and Esther as they stood watching.

A knot formed in her throat. Carriage wheels bumped against ruts in the path as they rode along in silence. The horses snorted and bobbed their heads, but Adelaide paid little heed.

"You all right?" Josiah asked.

"I'm fine."

"Look, Adelaide, I—"

She turned to him, and he stopped. "What is it, Josiah?" She wondered if he had changed his mind. "Would you rather I not go?"

Surprise lit his face. "What? No, of course not!"

The intensity of his words convinced her that at least he wanted her on the ship.

To cook.

He reached for her hand. "Thank you for saying yes."

"Why, it was my pleasure," she said. Then realizing she sounded a bit too bold, she quickly added, "I told you, I'd do just about anything to get to the sea."

"Of course." His lips drew into a thin line, and he jerked on the horses' reins. If Adelaide didn't know better, she would have thought she had disappointed him in some way, though she couldn't imagine why.

❧

"It's not supposed to be like this!" Josiah paced the floor of his bedroom while Adelaide freshened up in her room. He wrenched his fists into tight balls, then flexed them. His frustration grew with every step. What had he been thinking to ask Adelaide to be his wife only to serve as a cook for his ship? What kind of life was that for a woman? He'd taken advantage of her love for the sea just to fill a position on his ship. True, he had been a desperate man. After all, he couldn't sail without a cook. Still, he had been utterly unfair to her.

The vision of their wedding scene played upon his mind.

Adelaide's hair sneaking free of the pins and blowing in the breeze, dancing across her forehead and brushing lightly against her cheeks, her skin tinged pink by the chill, her eyes bright with hope. How could he look at her, knowing he had ruined her future?

"A business arrangement." Those had been his words.

His words.

Now he wished he could take them back. For her sake. *Stop it!* he told himself as he stood to pace once again. *She's making me go soft. I've got to stay away from her. Far away. She's here to cook. I'm helping her sail the seas; she's helping me keep my crew happy. It's as simple as that. Arranged marriages happen all the time. She wanted this as much as I did. We will live together. I will provide for her. We'll do just fine.* A dull ache knotted his stomach like a rusty chain. She'd agreed to a future with him, a life on the sea. So why did he feel guilty?

❧

Adelaide slipped into the front room of their home and waited for Josiah to enter. After what seemed an eternity, the bedroom door squeaked open.

"I'm loading the *Courage* with our things. I need to finalize everything for the voyage. The crew will be boarding soon. I'll stay on the ship tonight and get it in order." He glanced out the window. "Although it's our wedding night, the crew will think nothing of my being there since our departure is set for day after tomorrow." His words were gruff and curt.

Adelaide stared at him, speechless.

Grabbing the first box within reach, he lifted it into his arms and headed out the door.

Well, the least he could have done was let her spend another night with Ma and Esther. Now she would spend her wedding night alone. Humiliation washed over her. *You're an idiot, Adelaide! What did you think—you would pass the hours laughing and talking with your new friend? You're his wife in name only. A hired cook. Your pay is the sea. You've finally gotten what you've always wanted.* Tears stung her eyes. In a moment, her stubborn side kicked in. No! She would not wallow in self-pity. She had made this choice, and she would make the best of it. Isn't that what she had always done?

Although Adelaide stitched other people's clothes to help with the family income, when her pa died, she also had gone to work at the general store. Between the chores on the homestead, mending for others, and working at the store, Adelaide dropped into bed each night and quickly slipped into dreams of a different world. A world filled with adventure, foreign lands, and different cultures. Though the dreams gave her hope, despair threatened many a day. She feared she would live out her days in Yorksville. The idea had almost suffocated her.

So now she should be happy. Adelaide threw a pillow across the couch. She was feeling sorry for herself, and that was not like her.

For a moment, she sat in utter silence. Her heartfelt prayer started with tears. Finally, she began to speak. "Father, Thou art able to do all things. I ask not of Thee to change the life I have made for myself. I ask only for strength to carry on and make the best of the choices I have made. And above all, may I give all glory and honor to Thee alone for all Thy mercies extended to me. Amen."

Adelaide brushed away tears from her cheeks with the backs of her hands, then dabbed at her face with the material from her dress. Lifting her chin, she decided she would get through this. There would be no loneliness; the sea would be her constant companion.

She looked up to see Josiah coming toward the house. Just as he entered the door, she rose from the couch. Adelaide took a deep breath. "Let me help you, Josiah," she said in her kindest voice.

And what surprised her most was that she meant it.

five

Once he arrived at the *Courage*, Josiah checked through the shipping papers again. He decided he had the needed legal documents for all signed-up crewmen. He placed the stack of papers inside his desk.

Glancing once more through the inventory in the logbook, Josiah decided they had what they needed for the trip until they reached the next port. The food was loaded and ready to go. Potatoes and vegetables filled the goose pen. Heavy casks of beef, pork, hard bread, flour, and water spotted the deck and cookhouse.

Josiah walked through the lower deck and did a final check on the livestock. Squealing pigs, hogs, chickens, and bleating sheep restlessly shuffled about in the animal pens. Checking the livestock's food supply, Josiah scribbled some notes on the log that his first mate would be taking over. Everything seemed in order.

Finally, Josiah arrived in his cabin, tired and spent. He glanced around the quarters. His cabin and adjoining room together didn't match the size of the most modest of New England parlors. In a corner of the room sat a tiny privy. One of the few comforts of being a captain.

The skylight and a small stern window provided some lighting. Not much, but better than nothing. He shrugged. The size of the room, with slivers of glimpses into the sea world, had not bothered him. Until now. Could Adelaide live in such confined spaces? She hadn't seemed to mind when she'd seen it earlier in the day. He shouldn't worry, he told himself. After all, she wanted to sail the seas. A whaling ship was no place for coddling.

He wondered how he could be tough as nails in his role as a sea captain, lately when he thought of Adelaide, his strength turned to limp seaweed. He couldn't help feeling he had taken advantage of her. Still, she said this was what she wanted.

Once more, he looked around the cramped room. It didn't help that they had to have the stove in the room due to the cold. When they headed into warmer climates, they could remove it.

Adelaide could keep one trunk in the room if she chose to do so. It could serve as a table or bench and also be used for storage. Some things could be stuffed in the three drawers beneath the bed, but the rest of her trunks would be stowed in the ship's hold.

Although the room had little space to spare, Josiah would have to hang another bed before Adelaide arrived. For her privacy, he'd also hang a sheet of some kind between them.

Bothersome thoughts poked tiny holes into his peace of mind like determined mosquitoes. Josiah prepared for bed. Once settled under the covers, he willed himself to get needed sleep. Quieting the restless voices inside his head, he managed to shove away all thoughts but one. Could Adelaide build a happy life for herself here?

ॐ

The next morning, Josiah collected Adelaide and her things and brought them to the ship. After he'd seen to having her things put away, he busied himself with the tasks of a sea captain, but Adelaide stood on the wharf and drank in her surroundings. The men buzzed around the ship in a whir of activity. She marveled that this time she would not only watch the ship leave, she would be on it! Even if she and Josiah only pretended to have a marriage in front of others, Adelaide decided to make the most of this time and enjoy her seafaring life.

She knew the morning of November 28, 1856, would go down in her memory for years to come. Her first day to set sail. No doubt her grandchildren would one day discuss it. The thought warmed her before she realized there would be no grandchildren. She would not allow her thoughts to go there, not now. Nothing would spoil this day.

"Adelaide!"

Hearing a familiar voice but not quite placing it, Adelaide turned around. "Adam Bowman," she said with surprise. "What are you doing here?"

"I've signed on as first mate." Pride filled his voice.

Adelaide thought how proud Esther would be of him. Though Adam was three years older, he and Esther had hit it off from the day his family moved to town. In the past five years, they had written to one another while he was at sea, though communication was minimal. He stopped to see her whenever he was in port. Ma tried to discourage the friendship. She didn't like having anyone who had to do with whaling associate with her daughters.

"Congratulations! We didn't know you were in town. I'm surprised you didn't stop by the house. Esther will be disappointed!" Adelaide threw him a teasing grin.

He frowned. "I had only returned from a whaling trip when I learned my grandma had died. We went to Bayview and have just returned."

"Oh, I'm sorry."

He shrugged. "She was ready, though we didn't want to let her go." He shoved his hands into his trousers' pockets. "Then I'd signed up for the *Courage* and had to hurry back." He looked at her. "I wish I'd had more time. I wanted to see Esther. Wasn't sure if she had anyone special in her life, what with me gone all the time. I would have said good-bye to her if I'd known I still had a chance." He said the last phrase more as a question.

Adelaide picked up on it. "I believe you do," she encouraged. She noticed his ears turned lobster red.

"What are you doing here, anyway?"

She swallowed. "Well, uh, I got married yesterday to the captain of this ship." She tried to make the words sound as happy as a new bride.

"What?"

Adelaide thought Adam looked as though he'd choked on a fish bone. She laughed. "See what happens when you're away?"

"You've got a lot of explaining to do, young lady," he teased in a brotherly fashion.

"Mate," Josiah's deep voice interrupted, "I think you'd better get your things in order."

Adam looked at Josiah, then back to Adelaide. "Yes, Captain," Adam replied before quickly complying with orders.

Josiah's behavior left Adelaide mute.

"Adelaide, if you will please follow me." His voice was short and curt, leaving no room for comment.

Adelaide felt like a little girl being reprimanded by the schoolmaster. She couldn't imagine what she must have done wrong.

Once they reached the cabin, Josiah closed the door behind them. Adelaide opened her mouth to speak, but he cut her short.

"You must conduct yourself as a woman of propriety, Adelaide. These are rough characters you will be traveling alongside, and you'd do well to steer clear of the lot of them."

For a moment, disbelief caused her tongue to stick to the roof of her mouth. Though his remarks hurt and angered her, the concern in his voice pushed the sting of the insult at a distance. Oh, how she wished Esther's starry-eyed ways hadn't affected her. On the other hand, Adelaide did want Josiah to know, under no uncertain terms, that she was a decent woman.

Without conscious effort, she lifted her chin. "Captain Buchanan, as you get to know me, you will find I am a woman of propriety and conduct myself in such a manner. Further, I wish you to understand that I know that young man. Your first mate, Adam Bowman, happens to be a dear friend of our family." The words were measured and meted out evenly. She hoped Josiah would see he had jumped to a wrong conclusion.

His eyes narrowed. "All the more reason to steer clear, *Mrs.* Buchanan. Wouldn't want the crew to get the wrong idea." With that, he turned, walked through the door, and closed it hard, leaving Adelaide to stare behind him.

What had gotten into him? What had happened to the kind, gentle man she had been seeing for the past several weeks? Adelaide unlatched her trunk and began to rip things from inside and throw them onto the bed. "How dare he consider I would be less than a woman of propriety!"

Dresses, petticoats, books, paper, and underthings flew from her arms onto the cluttered bed. "Just because we're married doesn't mean he can tell me when and to whom I may speak." She didn't care that her underthings lay bare for anyone to see. "It would serve him right if he walked in right now. I'd love to embarrass him the way he embarrassed me!"

She pulled out her shoes and tossed one across the floor. Of course she was behaving as a child, but somehow she couldn't stop herself. It seemed since Josiah Buchanan had walked into her life and turned her world upside down, her emotions shifted with the eastern winds.

She threw herself into her clothes and started to whimper. Before she could work herself up into a good crying spell, she heard the door open. She shot up on the bed.

Josiah walked in and stared at her. For a moment, neither said a word. "I—" He stopped talking and glanced at the floor. Bending over, he picked up her petticoat and threw it on the bed. "You dropped something." He turned and walked right back out the door.

"Awgh!" she wailed before falling back into the pile of clothes on her bed.

❧

Later that evening, family and friends gathered aboard the

Courage in a final good-bye celebration. Together they enjoyed a fine feast, and then Adelaide and Josiah stood at the ship's rail, waving as whaleboats rowed their guests back to shore.

Once the excitement died down, the reality of her recent choices swept over Adelaide, filling her with a sense of melancholy. A quiet settled upon her as she pulled wide the curtain separating her bed from Josiah's.

Dressed for bed, she situated herself beneath the folds of blankets and quilts. Josiah's boots thumped against the floor, and she could hear him shrugging out of work clothes. She wished things could be different somehow. Their friendship had changed from the moment Josiah mentioned marriage. Things were now a bit, well, awkward between them. Adelaide took a deep breath and blew out a quick puff of air, snuffing the light from her lantern.

Josiah's bed shifted as she heard him climb in. He scooted about, then blew out his lantern.

Adelaide stared into the darkness. A sense of loneliness filled the tiny room. Heavy waves rocked the hull, but sleep escaped her. She heard Josiah turn restlessly on his bed and wondered if he stared blankly through the darkness, too.

આ

By the next morning, Adelaide's mood had improved considerably. She dressed quickly and pulled on her cape. When she opened the door, Josiah stood waiting on the other side.

"I thought I'd walk with you to the cookhouse."

Adelaide smiled and felt pleasure at the protective hand at her elbow, guiding her to her new workstation. The wooden deck sparkled from the cleaning it had received in port. Adelaide secured the top button on her cape against the eastward wind.

Once in the cookhouse, she quickly prepared a breakfast of eggs, coffee, and ham for herself, Josiah, and his mates. Although somewhat out of the ordinary, Josiah allowed the skilled members of his crew, such as the blacksmith and cooper or cask maker, as the position was sometimes called, to also join them in their cabin for meals. Adelaide knew that on most ships, the skilled workers ate after the captain and his mates. Josiah's kindness softened her heart toward him.

The rest of the crew sat on their sea chests on the main deck and ate the hardtack and ham that Adelaide made for them. They ate below deck only during foul weather.

Breakfast was soon over, and Adelaide watched as the men went to their various posts with the fire of adventure in their eyes.

After she scrubbed the cookhouse clean, she went out on the deck. The *Courage* set sail down the bay. The old ship groaned as the wind pushed it toward the high seas. Adelaide wanted to take one last look at her homeland before it disappeared with the shoreline.

The moment was bittersweet. She knew she would miss her family and her town, but as the wind filled the sails, excitement shot through her. She was living her dream.

As she made her way to the rail, sailors nodded cordial greetings, granting her the appropriate respect as befit a captain's wife. Adelaide edged closer to the rail to get a better view. Just then a sailor stepped in front of her. Deep lines rutted his forehead. Spiked whiskers poked through his jaw, reminding Adelaide of pins on a cushion.

"You want to be careful not to get too close to the ship's rail, ma'am," he said with a smile, revealing rotted teeth. He tipped his cap in a mock gesture that made Adelaide's skin crawl. No doubt the man had made his way through life bullying others. It was probably the only life he had ever known. She knew she couldn't show her fear, or she'd be miserable the rest of the journey. They had to serve on the ship together, and he needed to know up front where she stood. God's love softened her fear, and compassion filled her.

Without a blink, her gaze fixed on his threatening one. "Why, I thank you kindly for your concern, Mister—"

His eyes narrowed. Adelaide felt quite delighted that she seemed to have caught him off guard. "Ebenezer. The name's Ebenezer," he growled before stepping aside from her path and moving on his way.

Adelaide stared after him for a moment to let him know she was not frightened in the least. Which, of course, was not true. Underneath her clothing, her legs trembled. She waited until he edged away at a comfortable distance, then turned her eyes toward the sea.

I thank Thee, Father, for helping me in that situation. Please help Ebenezer to know Thee as well. Amen.

She lifted her face to the sky and took a deep gulp of the fresh sea air. Sometimes, the strong smell of fish overpowered the docks, but out on the sea, the air held the tangy scent of salt.

Pa, if only you could see me now. I think it would please you to find me on a whaling ship. I can't wait to experience all the excitement you shared with me as a child. Your stories built dreams in me, Pa. This is a whole new world. A world alive with color, activity. . .and loneliness.

Where had that thought come from? She hadn't a chance to feel lonely here. Too much work to do. Besides, her pa had taught her to look at the bright side of things, and she did. The sea. She was riding the seas on a whaling ship as the wife of a grand sea captain. How could she complain?

She stood in the warmth of the sunshine and drank in the awesomeness of God, the handiwork of His creation. Her spirit held her steadfast in the warmth of worship.

☙

Josiah caught a glimpse of Adelaide standing at the rail. Her eyes were closed, her face lifted skyward. The sun's rays sprayed upon her, casting her in an ethereal glow. She looked like an angel. He stood transfixed, watching her. No doubt she was praying. He had heard her whispered prayer the night before. She pored over her Bible with such enthusiasm, as if she couldn't live without it.

How did people attain such a faith? Though on land he had been a regular attender, church was more of a gathering place for him. He considered himself a good man. Never saw the need to get religion, as some folks put it. Didn't really have the time. Oh, he gave God the respect He deserved. Being a sea captain, he could do no less. Josiah believed God to be the Creator of the universe. Beyond that, he hadn't really given much thought to the matter.

Then when he felt folks let him down after Catherine— well, he didn't want to think about that. Yet watching Adelaide made him wonder. Was there more to it than what he had thought?

"You sure have arranged for a fine cook, Captain."

Josiah turned with a start to find Adam Bowman standing beside him. "A fine cook and a fine wife, Bowman." Josiah didn't smile. His own actions made him even more cross. Why did he feel he had to defend his position with this man like two roosters in a cockfight?

Adam blinked. "Yes, sir. Though I don't think you 'arranged' for the wife," Adam said with lighthearted banter. He seemed oblivious to Josiah's bitterness.

Josiah cringed inwardly. He knew Adam had no clue of his marriage arrangement—or did he? Could Adelaide have told him?

"Yeah, I'll say. Mighty fine wife, Captain." Ebenezer Fallon joined the two men, his eyes filled with challenge.

This man meant trouble, no doubt about it.

"I can only wish the same for you two in the future. Now, we best get back to our posts."

Adam nodded and hurried away. Ebenezer shot one last glare at the captain, then turned away. He took slow, deliberate steps, as if to let the captain know he would do what he wanted, when he wanted.

Yes, Ebenezer Fallon spelled trouble.

six

The following week, a constant gale from the west tossed the ship around like a ball of yarn between a kitten's paws. Josiah had to admit he admired Adelaide's strength. Cloaked in all its treachery, the sea caused even the sturdiest sailors to weaken at times. Yet, although Adelaide suffered with seasickness, she didn't complain. She continued to cook for the crew, ate nothing herself, then scurried to their cabin for relief. Josiah found her amazing. His own experience had told him women reveled in complaining, so he found himself puzzled by her.

When finished with his review of the logbook, Josiah snapped it shut, yawned, and stretched.

Since it was only a few weeks from Christmas, his thoughts went to the scrimshaw upon which he had been working. He hoped Adelaide would like the jagging wheels he had carved for her. Now she could crimp her piecrusts with no problem. He'd like to make her a rolling pin later. With a shrug, he told himself, after all, she was his wife; he needed to give her something.

A nagging thought agitated him. Maybe he should have purchased a gift from a store, something a little more feminine. Catherine had always complained he never understood women. Perhaps she was right. He found whales more predictable. Staring at the sea, he allowed his thoughts to continue. Even now, the *Courage* steered toward Verdade, South America, but he hadn't planned to pull into port. They had whales to catch, and so far only a few cries of "There she blows" had called from the masthead, with little hope of a catch up to now.

Josiah gazed at the rising sun. Looking at the sea, he found

50

it hard to remember its anger of the past days. He hoped Adelaide would soon adjust to this new life.

"Good morning, Josiah." Adelaide's soft voice broke through his musings. He turned to her and nodded as she joined him at the railing.

"You're looking much better this morning," he said with more softness than he'd intended.

"Thank you. I'm quite better." A slight breeze pulled a strand of hair loose from her pins and brushed it against her cheek. Adelaide tucked it back into her bonnet.

"Good." Josiah cast Adelaide a sideways glance. Her dark brown eyes reminded him of the rich, deep soil of a freshly tilled meadow; her creamy skin, the silk of a cornstalk. A nice change from what he usually saw on his ship.

A noise shook him from his foolishness. He turned to see a chicken strutting and clucking behind them.

Adelaide laughed. "I feel right at home seeing the pigs and chickens running around the deck."

"They are a lively bunch," Josiah said with a grin. "Guess they don't know they'll be supper one day."

She laughed.

The sound made him feel lighter somehow. "You're doing a great job with the meals, Adelaide."

She turned a surprised look to him. "Thank you." Her eyelids lowered and a pink flush fanned her cheeks.

"Good morning, Adelaide. Captain." Adam Bowman greeted them with a smile.

Josiah stiffened. "Bowman," he returned, his voice hard and formal.

If Adam Bowman noticed the change in the captain, he didn't let on. "Beautiful morning, isn't it?" he continued with a pleasant smile. Before anyone could respond, he turned to Adelaide. "I haven't seen you around except at mealtime, Addie. You been feeling poorly?"

Oh, this man irritated Josiah. Still, Bowman stood there

smiling as if he hadn't a clue of the captain's feelings. Not only did Josiah not like the man's cordial ways, but Josiah clearly did not like Bowman's familiar tone with Adelaide. Calling her Addie should be reserved for those closest to her. A thought struck him. Was Bowman close to her? Adelaide said he was a friend of the family. Perhaps he had called on Adelaide, but her love for the sea had won out. His stomach knotted up like a rusty chain, and he was completely puzzled as to why.

"Bowman, you would do well to remember your place," Josiah rushed in. "You will address her as Mrs. Buchanan like every other crewman."

Adam looked chagrined. "Sorry, Captain. I forget that—"

"It's all right, Adam. Josiah—I mean, Captain Buchanan just wants to keep order—"

"I understand," he managed. Embarrassment flamed his face.

The softness in her voice toward this man caused Josiah's blood to boil like blubber in a try-pot. *She is my wife, after all.* His breath turned quick and shallow as he attempted to calm his anger. An uncomfortable silence fell upon them.

Adelaide looked at each man briefly. A slight shadow crossed her face. "I'd better get started on the meal." The softness of her words, her calming ways, turned Josiah's stomach upside down more than the roughest of gales. Frustration ran through him. Despite the fact theirs was a marriage of convenience, Adelaide was still his wife, and Adam Bowman would do well to remember his place.

Josiah turned and walked away. "I can't let that woman make me soft," he muttered under his breath. Chickens clucked and piglets squealed to get out of his path as his boots stomped hard across the rough planks.

❧

Adelaide diced through the vegetables with a little more force than necessary. She couldn't understand Josiah's harsh treatment of Adam. Something told her Adam could one day be a member of their family, judging by the way he talked about her sister. Adelaide wanted Josiah and Adam to get along. Of course, Josiah didn't think of her in that way. Would he ever feel like a part of her family? What did the future hold for them?

The knife sliced into the potato, but before Adelaide realized it, she nicked the tip of her finger. "Oh!" She grabbed her hand.

"Are you all right?" Behind her, Josiah grabbed a cloth and dashed to her side. She stood perfectly still while he held her bleeding hand and looked over the cut. He maneuvered the cloth around her finger, winding it tight to stop the bleeding. Once finished, he held her hand in his.

Adelaide wasn't sure what to do. She felt clumsy and very female for having made such a mistake. Her eyes glanced up. "I'm sorry; I should have—"

"Shh." His fingertips reached up and touched her lips. He stared into her eyes. "It's all right." Allowing his fingers to trail down her cheek, he tilted her face toward him. "I'm sorry you hurt yourself."

His eyes were so intense and kind. Like the Josiah she had met not so long ago. All sights and sounds drifted away. Her world consisted only of this moment.

Alone with Josiah.

What was happening, she didn't know. She feared the slightest movement could break the magic. She dared take a slight wisp of a breath. Josiah's gaze never left her face as he dipped his head toward her, his lips claiming her own. For one brief moment of bliss, Adelaide felt all the pleasures and wonder of a real kiss. Like a shared secret between two people who loved each other from the depths of their souls.

Yet just as quickly as the moment commenced, it stopped. Josiah broke away, his body stiff and professional once again. "I'm sorry, Adelaide. I don't know what came over me." He looked down at the floor, then back to her. "It won't happen again." He turned on his heels and quickly left the cookhouse.

Adelaide stared after him, her trembling fingers tracing where his lips had been. Now that was something she hadn't seen coming. By the look on Josiah's face, she figured he hadn't planned on it, either.

She wasn't sure how she felt about what had happened. She only knew things were definitely changing between them. And where this change would take them, she could only imagine. . . .

❧

Josiah couldn't, for the life of him, figure out what had possessed him to kiss Adelaide. After he had promised himself he would stay away from her, not allow her to make him go soft, he had betrayed himself and spoiled everything. She would want nothing to do with him now, of that he felt sure.

She came along for an adventure at sea, not a romantic life with him. He shoved his fingers through his hair. He could kick himself.

Admittedly, he'd never met anyone like Adelaide. She was so complex, tougher to understand than most women. Determined, that's what she was. After all, it took a determined woman to handle life on a ship with a group of crusty whalers. But more than that, she was soft. Like a gentle breeze. Not just her skin, but her ways. She was unlike any woman he had ever seen. He couldn't put his finger on it. It was like she possessed a quiet strength from beyond herself.

Josiah raised his hands in frustration and let them drop at his side. Now he was thinking nonsense. A pig snorted at his feet, and Josiah growled at it, sending the poor creature off squealing.

Might as well admit it. You have feelings for her. The thought both surprised and angered him. Surprised him because he hadn't admitted it until now; angered him because he was accustomed to being in control of everything in his life. He felt as though his heart had committed mutiny against his better sense.

Josiah shook off the disturbing thoughts and walked through the ship, checking things, talking here and there with the crew. The men grew restless. Tension mounted daily. They were itching to kill a whale, and he knew it. They'd best find one soon.

Just as Josiah headed downstairs for the cabin to check on Adelaide, Adam's voice stopped Josiah short. Adam and the man to whom he spoke were hidden from Josiah's view.

"If I had known how she felt, I wouldn't be sailing on this ship today. I guess I've loved her since the day I met her." Adam's voice trailed to silence.

"Her father was Elijah Sanborn?" the other voice asked.

"Yeah, he's the one."

Sickness balled up in the pit of Josiah's stomach. He didn't hear the rest of the conversation. He had to get away. Never had the ship seemed so small. Going back on deck, he considered their chart. They would stop at Verdade, most likely arriving near Christmas Day. If the men grumbled, so be it. No matter the cost, he had to get away for a while, away from Adelaide. He needed to think.

❧

Adelaide situated her chair on the ship's deck. A glorious sun had risen over the waters. *Perfect for the Lord's Day,* she thought. She lifted her face to its rays. After a moment of sheer basking in the warmth, she pulled open her Bible and flipped to her reading for the day in Psalm 139. Her heart absorbed what her eyes told her. When she came to verses seven through ten, she stopped and reread the passage:

> *Whither shall I go from thy spirit? or whither shall I flee from thy presence? If I ascend up into heaven, thou art there: if I make my bed in hell, behold, thou art there. If I take the wings of the morning, and dwell in the uttermost parts of the sea; even there shall thy hand lead me, and thy right hand shall hold me.*

The passage wrapped itself around her heart like a warm embrace from God. Regardless of the circumstances, she was not alone. God would never leave her. Though her choices had brought difficulties, God would see her through. No matter how far from home, she was never out of His care. The thought brought tears to her eyes. "Oh, God, Thy mercy is never-ending." She felt her heart nearly burst with praise.

Overcome with worship, her voice lifted with the melody "I Sing the Mighty Power of God."

Footsteps sounded behind her, but before the melodies stopped in her throat, a couple of male voices joined in.

Adelaide turned in pleasant surprise to see Adam and another crewman, whose name she couldn't remember, standing beside her, smiling. The three turned toward the sea and lifted their voices in further praise as they finished the rest of the song. Other sailors eyed them curiously.

When the song ended, Adam was the first to speak. "Would you share a Scripture with us, Ad—Mrs. Buchanan?" he quickly corrected himself.

Adelaide smiled and threw him an I'm-sorry-you-have-to-call-me-that look. She nodded and looked at her Bible. Lifting it to her, she began to read Psalm 139. So engrossed was she in the Scripture, she hadn't noticed the footsteps surrounding her. By the time she had finished, three-fourths of the crew circled her.

Not sure what to do from there, Adelaide felt she must not let the opportunity go unheeded. Whispering a quick prayer in her heart for the right words, she told the sailors that everyone had sinned and fallen short of the glory of God. She shared the message of God's love for each of them and told them how He sent His Son to die in their place. Further, she explained that because of God's provision through His Son, those who believed in Him would not perish but would have eternal life. Some of the crew shifted uneasily where they stood.

Quickly, Adelaide lifted her voice in a prayer for each of

them. When the prayer was over, only a few had walked away. The others who lingered, she noticed, had removed their caps and simply stood in the warmth of the sunshine.

Greatly encouraged, she started singing "O, For a Thousand Tongues to Sing." Adam quickly joined in, and a couple of others soon followed. Though the song had been out a few years, the burly crew had probably not been exposed much to songs of faith.

At the back of the crowd, Adelaide spotted a man with cap in hand. He seemed clearly moved by their little service. His sad gaze caught hers, and he turned and walked away. She wanted to call after him but knew the time wasn't right. Oh, how she wanted to know more about this man of mystery.

Captain Josiah Buchanan.

seven

Adelaide felt lighthearted after sharing Scriptures and songs with some of the crew, although she couldn't ignore the pain stabbing her heart each time she thought of the look on Josiah's face. What troubled him? Maybe the Lord had been talking to him. Perhaps a painful past plagued him. Did he regret marrying her because he still loved his first wife? Could Adelaide make him forget Catherine? Did Adelaide want to? She had to admit to herself she had growing feelings for this man. Could he ever make room in his heart for her?

Adelaide went to the cookhouse and fixed mutton stew for lunch from leftovers. One thing she had already learned in her brief stay on the *Courage:* No food was wasted on a ship. She stirred the pot of vegetables and cut up the bread she had made earlier that morning.

Sometimes Josiah and Adelaide ate in their room alone while the officers ate in the adjoining cabin. Today was such a day. Josiah joined Adelaide for lunch. She arranged the bowls nicely on her trunk, managing even a little candlelight between them. Though the sun crept through the porthole, she thought the candle might make Josiah more comfortable.

She watched as he picked up his spoon. She quickly bowed her head and said grace for them both. Afraid to look up when she was finished, she picked up her spoon and started eating, feeling his gaze upon her.

"You have a beautiful voice."

She dropped her spoon and splashed broth upon her dress. "Oh, dear." She wiped at the offensive stain with her cloth napkin. "I'm so clumsy." Her face grew warm.

"I said, you have a beautiful voice."

His compliment ran clear through her like warm cream on a cold winter's night.

"Adelaide, would you look at me, please?"

She swallowed and looked at him.

"Your voice. It's beautiful." He extended his hand to her. "I had no idea you could sing like that."

She struggled to get the last bite of vegetables down her throat. Things were definitely changing between them. With another swallow, she finally managed to murmur, "Thank you."

Josiah looked down at his hand, and as if he suddenly realized he was holding hers, he quickly pulled it away.

Adelaide tried to ease the disappointment squeezing her heart.

He picked up his spoon. "My ma used to sing like that."

Adelaide's head jerked up. Josiah never talked about his family to her. All of a sudden, she realized how little she knew about him. She watched him as he stared into his soup bowl, seeming to catch a glimpse of days long ago.

"Tell me about your ma."

He shrugged and looked at her. "Not much to tell, really." Lifting his spoon to his mouth, he took another bite.

Adelaide feared she had broken their moment of sharing, but he continued. "Pa was the captain of a whaling ship; did I tell you that?"

She shook her head, praying he would tell her more.

"Ma pretty much raised me alone in Bayview. Pa was always at sea. I hardly knew him." Josiah drank some water. "For a while, she cried herself to sleep most every night. I can't say for sure when she finally stopped." He scratched his face thoughtfully. "We did all right. Pa sent money home for us. Then Ma got sick when I was fourteen. Died of the fever. I didn't know what to do. Had no other family. So I did what seemed natural. Signed up on a whaling ship. Course, I started out as a cabin boy. By the time I was eighteen, I was an experienced whaleman. Then I worked my way up to harpooner and eventually on up to captain. I guess it's all the life I've ever known." He looked at her. "Can't help but think Ma wouldn't like it, though."

"What happened to your pa?"

"Don't know. When Ma died, I just moved on to whaling. Never knew how to find him after that."

"Oh, Josiah, I'm sorry."

He tipped his head. "That's the way life is out here." He suddenly looked at her as if he'd maybe said too much. "I hope I'm not scaring you about life on the sea." He seemed to almost hold his breath.

Adelaide smiled. "No. Though I've never been on a ship before, I'm aware of some of the struggles."

Josiah settled back into his seat as if he felt much relieved.

"I want to thank you for having the men slaughter the animals for our meals. That's one thing I don't enjoy. It's a chore I had to do at home, of course, but I'm thankful for the help here."

"It's called survival. You're too tender for your own good." Josiah's words were gruff, but she could feel the kindness behind them.

"I suppose you're right. But I thank you just the same."

He nodded, finished his last bite of lunch, then stood to go. He turned to her. "That little service you had this morning—good for the men. You can do it every week if you want."

Adelaide nodded. Excitement shot through her with the idea of such an opportunity. "Thank you, Josiah." Did she see a half smile touch his lips before he turned to go?

Josiah closed the door behind him. Adelaide settled back into her chair. She clapped her hands together. "Yes, Father, Thy mercy is never-ending."

≈

The next two weeks were fairly uneventful, but for the rough, strong winds, much to Josiah's dismay. Though a few whales had been spotted, there had been nothing close enough to chase. They'd caught a porpoise or two and a few blackfish, storing away what oil they could. But he hoped they'd spot a whale soon.

Josiah had made his rounds on the ship and sat at a bench, whittling on scrimshaw for Adelaide. The gales had tossed the ship long enough, and now a pleasant breeze settled upon him, just warm enough for comfort.

All of a sudden, a flying fish plopped on the deck. A couple of men laughed, then ran over to scoop it up. For Adelaide, no doubt. Flying fish were plenty. Adelaide had cooked some for breakfast. Josiah thought the way Adelaide prepared it, the fish tasted like fresh herring. A smidgen of pride overtook him for having the foresight to ask her to be their cook. Course, he knew now he wanted her for more than a cook, but that hadn't been part of their agreement. She would cook and enjoy life on the sea. He would enjoy a happy crew and good meals. Oh, how he wished he could turn back the clock. He wondered how things might have played out had there been time for courting.

What was he thinking? He had been burned once by the fickleness of a woman; did he want to go through that again? He had given his heart, only to have it smashed like a ship wrecked upon rocky shores. A part of him wanted to believe Adelaide was different. Yet another part of him warned him to stay away. He couldn't account for others, only himself. He had to make it on his own.

Besides, even if she did fall in love with him, what could he offer her? Oh, she liked the ship now, but a year from now? Three years? What then? What about children? Though he knew some captains took their families aboard the whaling ship, he didn't want that for his family. That would leave Adelaide to raise the children on land. Alone. Just like him and his ma.

If only they would spot a whale, he could keep busy and forget all the nonsense clouding his thoughts. His jackknife gouged deep into the whalebone as Josiah worked with determination to shape it into a rolling pin. Though he knew he wouldn't have it done by Christmas, he figured he could give it to Adelaide later.

Christmas. They would be upon Verdade soon. The crew was restless, and a stop in the port would do them all good. He kept his eyes on Ebenezer. He didn't like what he saw. Seemed each time Josiah passed Ebenezer, the man was whispering to other crewmen, only to stop abruptly when Josiah walked by. What was so secret? Josiah couldn't trust the man, of that he was sure.

No, he'd better get the crew to port before Ebenezer stirred them up into a disgruntled lot.

❧

With breakfast over, Adelaide settled down to work on the unfinished shirt she was putting together for Josiah. She hadn't had much chance to sew since she'd spent so much time in the cookhouse. Her fingers ran over the material appreciatively. She hoped Josiah would like it. It hadn't been easy to keep it from him. After all, she didn't want to spoil his Christmas surprise.

With great concentration, she worked on the shirt, adding a few final touches as needed. Before she knew it, the time had come to prepare lunch. She flipped out the shirt before her and looked at the handiwork with pleasure. It turned out all right. She hoped Josiah thought so. Folding it neatly in place, Adelaide tucked the gift carefully in her drawer in a space emptied for it.

Just then, their door swung open. "A whale's been spotted. "We're going out." Excitement filled Josiah's words, while a touch of fear settled upon Adelaide. With the news delivered, Josiah disappeared behind the closed door.

Adelaide could hear the crew thunder across the deck above. She put away her things and hurried up to watch the excitement.

The crew scurried across the deck in a frenzy of commotion.

Tubs of harpoon line were quickly hoisted into the three whaleboats. Josiah, Adam, and the second mate, Benjamin West, took their positions at the steering oars in the stern of their respective whaleboats, and the boatsteerers manned the harpooner's oar in the bows. The twelve oarsmen remained on deck and lowered the boats into the water. Once the boats floated beside the ship, the oarsmen climbed down the sides of the ship, and four men each crowded into their assigned boat.

Though Adelaide knew this was the reason they had come, she couldn't prevent the concern that shadowed her heart. Not only did she care about Josiah, but she cared about the souls of his crew.

Breathing a prayer, Adelaide continued to watch the busy crew at work. Maybe this would be the day they would catch a whale. Josiah had thought perhaps they could stop at Verdade, but if they caught a whale, most likely, they would sail on. She had hoped to step foot on land and browse through some shops, but then that was selfish thinking on her part. Once again, she found herself praying for the men.

When the boats were out a distance, bobbing on the swells, Adelaide went to the cookhouse to prepare dinner. With no lunch in their stomachs, the men would be hungry when they returned.

Though the owners of the *Courage* provided little extra provisions for the sailors, Adelaide knew Josiah surrendered some of his wages to grant his crew better eating. Most sailors' meals consisted of nothing more than hardtack— biscuits so hard, they could break a man's teeth—and a hunk of salt beef or pork with an occasional dumpling thrown in. Though sometimes the men had to eat such meals, and the common sailor didn't eat quite the fare of that of the officers, Josiah still saw to it that they ate a decent meal as often as possible. He insisted the success of a whaling ship depended on his crew's health.

After sticking a chicken in the oven to roast with some

potatoes and carrots, Adelaide prepared some bread for baking for the officers. She then prepared salt pork with a small serving of potatoes for the rest of the crew. She would also set aside some bread for them. With the chicken cooking in the oven, she slipped back on deck. By then, the whaleboats were merely a speck on the horizon.

· Adelaide decided to go to the cabin to pray and read her Bible for a while. Later, she went back to check on the chicken and to stick the bread in the oven. By the time she returned to the deck, low-flying clouds hung from the sky like a lumpy mattress. Day had surrendered to night. An eerie feel settled upon the ship and covered Adelaide with shivers. She tried to rub the chill from her arms.

"No use to fret none, Miss Adelaide."

Adelaide spun on her heels. Who would dare call her that after Josiah had given strict instructions not to do so? She turned to see Ebenezer. He looked sickly, his eyes bloodshot, his nose as red as a boil.

Knowing Ebenezer's job was oarsman on Benjamin's whaleboat, Adelaide asked, "Wha–what are you doing here?"

"Now is that any way to treat a man who's been seasick?" He pulled a bottle from his back pocket, took a drink, and swiped his mouth with the back of his hand. ·

Adelaide felt fear climb her spine. Her gaze swept across the deck in search of help. She didn't see the three shipkeepers who were supposed to stay behind and handle the ship.

"Oh, one of the men filled in for me. I'm sick, you know." A wicked grin heightened his evil expression. "The other two are in the cookhouse, helping themselves to your fine food."

Her head jerked around toward the cookhouse. She thought she heard distant sounds of the crew returning to the ship, but Ebenezer's hearing appeared dulled by his drink. He didn't flinch.

"I hope you don't mind," he said with insincerity. "I told them you said to eat so they would have strength when the rest of the crew returned." His lip curled into a snarl. "I'd like to help myself to a little dessert."

Adelaide gasped.

Before another moment passed, sounds of the crew climbing back up the ship came from the starboard side. Ebenezer turned with a start, searching frantically for a place to deposit his bottle. Adelaide drew a shuddering breath and watched as he ran off the deck and down the stairs. Shaken but unharmed, she turned her attention toward the returning crew.

Adelaide's heart lightened with the sight of Josiah. He came right to her. The uncomely sight before her took her breath away, but the excitement on his face lessened the trauma.

"We caught a fin. Not the biggest whale, but a whale, nonetheless."

She thought he was going to slap her on the back, but he stopped his hand midair. Her nose wrinkled with the smell.

Josiah laughed. "Sorry, but you'll get used to it. Hopefully, you'll see more than this in the days ahead."

Activity swirled around her. Wood was thrown beneath the try-pots where a fire soon commenced. Adelaide stood out of the way and watched the process with fascination. Blubber was cut into pieces and placed into the heavy iron pots. Crispy scrap pieces floated to the surface of the pot and were skimmed off, then tossed into the fire for more fuel. The smell of the burning scraps created a black smoke and an unforgettable stench.

Adelaide pinched her nose to squelch the foul odor. She turned a glance toward the bloodstains, the huge masses of flesh and blubber soaking the pine-timbered deck, and decided not to announce dinner. With her hand held tight against her stomach, she slid through the greasy planks for her cabin.

"You chose this life, Adelaide Buchanan," she told herself. "You and you alone."

Her swift, uneasy footsteps carried her to the cabin, where she arrived at the privy just in time.

eight

Adelaide couldn't believe it. She had always dreamed of a whaling ship, and here she was sick at the sight of a catch! The very idea. Her pa would be shocked. She wiped her mouth with a cloth, feeling ashamed beyond belief.

She'd never seen such a sight. That thought helped justify her illness. Such a massive creature. Why, the mere sight of it took her breath away. Josiah was right. She was too tender. One look at the dying creature turned her insides soft. A nurturing instinct told her to run to the whale, defend it, nurse it to health. But, of course, the killing wasn't for sport but rather the good of mankind. A necessity. At least that's what she had always heard. Yet after seeing the whale. . .

Enough of that, she told herself, attempting to calm her stomach.

Adelaide walked over to the drawer that held her journal and slipped it out. Before writing, her thoughts went to Ebenezer. She hadn't told Josiah of the earlier episode. She felt Ebenezer didn't want a woman on the ship and hoped to stir up trouble for Josiah. Well, she decided, she wouldn't give Ebenezer the satisfaction. It seemed best to keep the matter hidden.

Adelaide settled in the chair and began to write in her journal of her experience as she had done every day since boarding the ship.

Once she finished, Adelaide pulled out some paper and began a letter to Ma and Esther. Though she'd have to wait awhile before mailing them, Adelaide decided to write and store up her letters for when they reached a port or visited a passing ship. She would send the letters all at once.

Adelaide kept her news lighthearted and happy to keep Ma from worrying. She told Ma and Esther of the beauty of the sea, the adventurous gales, as she put it, and of her work on the ship. Although Esther had been sick when the *Courage* set sail and she had missed seeing Adam, Adelaide kept her sister informed on how things were going. The mere mention of his name would no doubt set Esther's heart to flutter.

Adelaide thought for a moment. Oh, how she did miss her little family. If only she could hug them once more.

By the time Adelaide had finished writing to Ma, Esther, and the Markles, she was tired and spent. She had hoped to do laundry the following day but knew everything would be at a standstill until the final cask of oil was stowed away below deck.

She prepared for bed and slipped under the covers. She had pulled the sheet on the wall for privacy when Josiah walked in.

"Adelaide, are you still awake?"

She shot up in bed. "Yes, Josiah."

"May I come around?"

She pulled her covers up around her shoulders. "Yes," she said before gulping. Though she felt ashamed for thinking it, she'd hoped he had cleaned up a little before coming to her.

He had.

"I think things are pretty much under control. The try-pots are heavy with boiling oil, and the last of the blubber has been minced into small pieces, waiting their turn in the pots."

"Will the men have to stay up late to finish things?"

He nodded. "We have try watches, five to six hours long. They'll get little sleep." He rubbed his chin. "The oil has to be tried out, then put into casks, cooled, and stowed away for market. Then the ship has to be scrubbed clean. I thought you might want to get in the flour barrels and roll out some doughnuts in the morning—you know, cook them in the scalding oil. That oil will be as sweet as new hog's lard."

"All right, I'll do that." She smiled. He was always thinking of the crew.

"We've all been snitching a bite of dinner here and there. Thank you. It sure was tasty."

She stared at Josiah. His words ran together like an excited schoolboy. Her heart constricted. She found his enthusiasm endearing. "You're welcome."

He looked at her, then at his hands. He shoved them in his pockets like he didn't know what else to do with them. "Well, I just wanted to make sure you were all right. You'd never seen a catch before, had you?"

She shook her head.

"You're amazing. Most women would get sick with the sight. You're my strong one, Adelaide. Good night." With that, he turned and left.

Guilt covered her. It's not like she'd had the chance to tell him she had gotten sick, or so she told herself. She lifted her chin. Well, next time she felt quite sure she would be just fine. Each time would get easier.

She settled back into bed and snuggled into her pillow. Closing her eyes, she played back his words. *You're amazing. You're my strong one, Adelaide.* Her eyes popped open. The words played once more. *You're my strong one, Adelaide.* Into the darkness, she whispered, "He said 'my' strong one." A smile touched her lips. Somehow she liked the sound of that.

❧

Adelaide stretched into the darkness. Though she was tired from the past few days of working around the men as they prepared the captured whale, the excitement of Christmas morning rushed through her like a child. She was delighted Josiah had decided to stop in Verdade. He said the men needed the break. On land, they could celebrate the good fortune of capturing their first whale. They would arrive tomorrow, and Adelaide could hardly wait.

Quietly, she slipped from her bed in hopes of not disturbing

Josiah. She wanted to get an early start in the cookhouse.

She had plans of a special Christmas lunch for the men. Not just the officers—she meant every crewman to enjoy this meal. Mentally, she went through her list. She would prepare stuffed roast chickens, potatoes, stewed cranberries, cucumbers, bread with jam, and squash. For dessert, mince pie. Coffee, tea, and water to drink. And the best of all, she'd prepared popcorn balls for each of the crewmen. The anticipation filled her. With swift motions, she dressed for the day.

While she dressed, the door of their room opened, giving her a start. "You awake, Adelaide?" Josiah's voice called to her.

She smiled. So he had already started his day. It was she who had slept too long. "Yes, Josiah, I'm awake." Smoothing out her skirt, she pulled open the curtain to see him. A smile flashed across his eyes and lit upon his mouth. The way he looked at her made her feel he approved of her appearance.

"Merry Christmas." His eyes twinkled.

She almost wanted to giggle. Christmas seemed to bring that out in people.

"I have a gift for you. Do you want it now or after breakfast?"

Adelaide couldn't hide her pleasure. She felt most happy he had thought to give her something. "After breakfast, if that's all right. We'll have more time to enjoy it then."

He nodded as if appreciating her good sense. "You ready to go?"

"Yes."

He held out his arm to escort her, and suddenly it seemed to her they were back at the church social as he prepared to escort her out to the beach where he had asked her to marry him—or more precisely, to be his cook. No matter what their original intentions had been, things were changing between them, and for that she was thankful. To top it all off, today was Christmas.

The officers ate breakfast in their cabins, while Josiah and Adelaide brought their meals back to their room, and the men ate on deck.

"Delicious meal, as always, Adelaide." Josiah wiped his mouth with the cloth napkin she had sewn before they were wed. He had eaten his meal so quickly, Adelaide wondered how he even had time to taste it.

"Time for your gift." Josiah stood.

Adelaide reached out and touched his arm. "Josiah, would you mind terribly if we read the Christmas story together first?"

Childlike disappointment flickered in his eyes. She smiled.

He tossed a halfhearted grin her way. "Oh, sure." He looked across the room for her Bible and went to fetch it. Picking up her Bible, he took it to her.

She turned to the appropriate passage in Luke and looked up at him. "Would you read, Josiah?" She held her breath, fearing what he would answer.

With a look of confusion, he reluctantly took the open Bible from her. "All right." He began to read the words. His bass voice sounded through the room as she closed her eyes and listened to the greatest story ever told. Her heart never tired of the story of the Savior's birth.

Josiah finished the passage, then handed it back to her.

"Thank you." She bowed her head and led them in a prayer of thankfulness that they could celebrate such a wonderful day and that she could share it with Josiah. She hadn't meant to say those last words. In fact, she felt mortified they had escaped her. What would he think of her now? Though she felt things were changing between them, he hadn't said things were different. As far as she knew, he still didn't want another wife. He wanted a cook. At least for now, that's the way she saw it. She turned grumpy. It was all Esther's fault.

Before her mood could grow any darker, she looked up at him. His eyes were shining. She decided he must not have heard the last part. Hadn't she said them in just barely a whisper? That was it. He hadn't heard her. Relief washed over her.

Josiah rubbed his hands together. "It's time?"

Adelaide laughed and nodded. "It's time."

While he went to his drawer and pulled out something for her, she went over to her own hiding place to pull out her gift to him.

They each walked back to one another and hid their presents behind their backs. Josiah looked at her in surprise, as if he hadn't considered that she might have a gift for him.

He cleared his throat. "I, uh, know how you like to cook and all. You bake tasty pies and work so hard to make them look nice." He pulled the gift from behind his back. "Well, I made you something."

Adelaide looked at the scrimshaw in his hand. "Jagging wheels! Oh, Josiah, now I can crimp my pie shells! Thank you!" Forgetting herself, she placed his present on the trunk behind her and reached over to hug him. Overcome with excitement, she hadn't realized the boldness of her behavior until she felt his arms firm around her back, holding her tight against him. She felt herself flush. Quickly, she pulled away and hurried back to her present.

She reached for his gift and handed it to him. "Thank you for your hard work and kindness."

He ran his fingers along the material, then looked at her. "You made this?"

She nodded.

"It's mighty fine," he said, looking at the shirt. He glanced back at her. "Mighty fine, indeed." A wide smile stretched across his face, causing her heart to tumble like a fish in a net.

"Merry Christmas, Addie."

❧

After lunch, the men came up to the deck where Josiah and Adelaide sat enjoying the calm sea. It seemed to her only fitting the Lord should provide a restful sea on Christmas. Though she had to admit she had never experienced such a warm Christmas. Not the slightest hint of a breeze stirred. The canvas sails didn't have a single kink. They wouldn't make much headway today. Adelaide pulled off her bonnet and tucked stray hairs from her neck back into her hairpins. She felt sticky.

The men seemed in good spirits. Many of them thanked her for the delicious meal that reminded them of home. Adam Bowman came up behind them and pulled out a harmonica, much to Adelaide's pleasure and surprise.

He started playing some Christmas tunes. Pretty soon, others gathered round, some laughing, some singing. Before she could blink, Josiah stood and left, taking all her joy right with him. Others watched him leave but kept right on singing.

They were having such a wonderful time together; why did he have to spoil it all? Well, she wouldn't allow him to ruin her Christmas. She joined in the singing once again.

The melodies floated over the ship and surrounding waters as they each sang from their hearts. Adelaide lifted her face to the sun and sang with gusto. Suddenly a strange sound hit her ears. She stopped singing and listened. Recognizing it, she turned to find Josiah standing nearby playing a fiddle. He smiled and winked at her. Much to her dismay, she let out the most unladylike laugh. She couldn't help herself.

More pleasure than she had ever known rushed through her. Could life get more wonderful than at this very moment? Once the singing stopped, they all laughed and made comments to Josiah and Adam about their great music. Pride washed over Adelaide as she watched Josiah.

Her husband.

A whaleman named John spoke up. "You know, I can remember one Christmas our pa was away from home. He had gone to a nearby town for some seed—and I suspect a present or two. A blizzard blew in on our little community, and on Christmas morning, Pa wasn't home. We kids sat around long-faced, even though Ma tried to cheer us up, presenting us with our stockings filled with an orange and a peppermint stick. Funny how even the candy didn't matter 'cause we were worried about Pa.

"I can still remember Ma's rocking chair as it rubbed against the wooden floor, back and forth, back and forth. The wind blew hard against our homestead, causing our only window to rattle. The clock on the mantel ticked away while my brothers and I scribbled on some paper at the table.

"All of a sudden, the door blew open. In walked Pa, covered from head to toe with snow and shivering like a nervous chicken." John let out a laugh, his thoughts still seemingly far away.

"Ma gasped and ran to his side, as did we boys. We helped get Pa by the fire. Ma stripped him down to his underwear, filled him with hot coffee, and had him good as new in no time. Then Pa grabbed his bag and pulled out some dress material for Ma and little horses carved from wood for me and my brothers.

"It was the best Christmas I ever had."

Smiles lit through the crowd, and one by one the rough old whaling crew shared their Christmas stories. Adelaide scratched her head in wonder of it all. Even the roughest of characters deep down had some good in them. She had to believe that. *God doesn't give up on us, so why should we give up on others? As long as there is breath, there's always hope.*

Her gaze fell upon Ebenezer. So much had happened since their encounter on the ship's deck, she hadn't even given it much thought. Yet now the sight of him made her cold. She adjusted the shawl on her shoulders. Just then he glanced at her and caught her staring. He sneered, then turned and walked away.

She watched him leave, remembering what Josiah had told her. It seemed Ebenezer had once been the captain of a ship. Something unfortunate had transpired on his journey. Josiah thought it had something to do with Ebenezer's drinking habit and some bad judgment, though Josiah wasn't sure of the details. Whatever the problem, it reduced Ebenezer from a captain to a mere worker on whaling ships. Bitterness ate away at his soul like alcohol ate away at his future.

There was always hope, she reminded herself. Even for one such as Ebenezer Fallon. Wasn't there? Still, the choice was his to make.

After the Christmas stories, the group sang a few more songs. Adam and Josiah joined in and played a couple of songs together. Adelaide thought they actually looked as though they were enjoying themselves. Maybe, just maybe, they could be friends, after all. What a wonderful day.

After dinner, Josiah walked Adelaide back to their room. "It's been a fine day, hasn't it?" Josiah asked as he helped her step through their door.

She untied the ribbon on her bonnet and straightened her hair. She turned to him. "It has been one of the best Christmases ever for me."

"Truly?" His eyes sparkled.

"Truly," she answered before staring at the bonnet in her hands.

"Tomorrow, Verdade."

She looked up with excitement. "I can hardly wait."

Josiah laughed when he looked at her. "I'm glad you're enjoying yourself, Adelaide."

She looked at him but said nothing.

"You're not sorry you've come?"

Her eyes went to her bonnet again as she shook her head.

Josiah walked over to her and lifted her chin. The very touch of his fingers against her skin made her tingle.

"I'm glad," he said. His finger traced the side of her hair; then his gaze pinned hers. "I'll bet your hair is pretty down, too."

Adelaide's heart thumped so hard in her chest, she thought sure he could hear it. Embarrassment told her to move, but her feet refused.

He stared at her, looking as though he would kiss her at any moment.

Then just as quickly as the moment had settled upon them, it left. Josiah blinked and pulled away. His voice took on a friendly yet distant manner. "Yes, I'm quite sure you'll like Verdade," he said as he turned and pulled out his nightclothes.

Adelaide said nothing. With Josiah at her side, she knew she could like anything.

nine

The next morning sparkled with promise. Adelaide quickly prepared skipjack for the crew for breakfast. Though not her favorite fish to eat, it did add variety to their daily meals.

Josiah entered the cookhouse. "We caught a porpoise."

Adelaide worked with the iron pot on her stove and turned to him. "Wonderful."

Josiah snitched a piece of skipjack. "Should get about two gallons of oil from the skin. Hopefully, that will be enough to keep us from darkness for a season until we can get some more."

Adelaide nodded. "I thought I would make sausage cakes for dinner, if that's all right."

Josiah nodded. "Good idea. They're as good as pork sausages." He paused a minute. "We'll pull into Verdade about noon today."

Adelaide felt excitement course through her. He must have seen it in her eyes.

"After lunch, I'd like to escort you through town to see some of the shops."

She eyed him closely. His clothes looked fresh, and he smelled as clean as a breeze. Without whiskers, his face looked as soft as baby skin. Her heart stirred.

"Addie?"

Oh, how she liked the way he said that. "I'm sorry, Josiah. Yes, I would like that very much."

"Good." He smiled. He was about to leave, then turned an anxious look to her. "We'll only be able to stay till nightfall. The men want to keep moving."

"I understand."

He tipped his head, then walked out.

Adelaide fluttered around the room with a light heart. She could hardly wait to step on land.

※

Josiah felt quite the lucky man as he escorted Adelaide through the streets of Verdade. He noticed more than one turned head as Adelaide walked past the men on the streets. He sneaked a glance at her. She had a natural beauty about her. He couldn't quite describe it. Like she glowed from the inside out. Catherine hadn't had that. Oh, she'd been pretty to look at, but something had been missing, though he couldn't say what. His heart clenched as he thought about Catherine. Not from love for her but from the pain she had caused him.

The more he thought about it, the more he wondered if the pain he had felt those first months after her leaving him was more from a hurt ego than from a love lost. He thought he had loved her, but then he'd never been in love before, so how could he be sure? The feelings growing in his heart for Adelaide were different than what he had felt for his first wife. Catherine had used her feminine ways on him, and before he knew it, he was caught like a fish on a line.

No matter. He didn't want to think ill of the dead. She had been his wife, after all, even if only for a short time.

Adelaide broke through his thoughts as they stepped past the wharf and onto the street dotted with a couple of shops. "Were you surprised some of the men didn't want to stop here?"

"You know, I was. I thought they'd like a break. But once a man gets whaling in his blood, it's hard to let it go. There's always that gnawing need to catch another. Just the same, I think we all needed the time here. I hope to do a little trading as well." He looked at her and smiled.

"It seems odd to have such hot weather near the end of December. Back home, we'd be bundled in heavy layers of wool by now."

Josiah cast a sideways glance at Adelaide as she patted a handkerchief against her forehead, just under the brim of her bonnet. "It is, indeed, warm. Would you like to stop here?" Josiah asked, pointing toward a cozy little dress shop.

"Oh, could we?"

How could he refuse when he saw that sparkle in her eyes? "Of course."

Inside, the room smelled sharp like the sea. Colorful bolts of cloth lined overhead shelves. Laces and ribbons of assorted shapes and sizes were arranged to entice the simplest of tastes. A small gathering of stylish hats and gloves stood in a corner. Oriental silks lined a table.

Adelaide walked over to the material and began to browse, feeling her way through each fabric.

Josiah watched the scene, an unfamiliar stir running through him. He meandered through the store, then turned to see Adelaide admiring a light blue gown and matching bonnet fringed with ruffles. He imagined Adelaide in such a gown and bonnet and decided she must have them.

He waited patiently as she looked around. Each time she seemed interested in an item, upon finding the price, she graciously declined. No doubt she didn't feel she could ask him for the money—probably because she knew they were only pretending at a marriage. Would she ever want it to be more?

Suddenly the bell rang on the front door, and Josiah turned to see Adam Bowman entering. Though Josiah fought against it, his muscles grew tense. He glanced at Adelaide, who hadn't yet noticed Adam.

Adam spotted Adelaide, but Josiah stayed somewhat hidden behind merchandise.

"Why, Adam, what are you doing in here?"

Josiah could hear the teasing in Adelaide's voice. He swallowed hard.

"I just thought I'd see if I could find something for my

girl." He grinned. "I've been saving money for quite some time, so I have a little."

Adelaide smiled at him as if they shared a secret.

Josiah felt raw nerves. Who did that man think he was? Had he no respect for the fact Adelaide was married? Or maybe she had explained it was a marriage of convenience. Did they have plans for a future together? Josiah clenched his fists. He took a deep breath and released his fingers, noticing his white knuckles.

Suddenly his heart felt heavy. The light of the day seemed to grow dim as his thoughts took a different direction. Adelaide and Adam continued in small talk, but Josiah turned away. He could hear no more.

"Josiah." Adelaide walked up behind him and touched his arm. "I'm ready to go if you are." Her words were soft and tender, somewhat soothing his angry heart.

Josiah glanced over his shoulder to see Adam watching them. Josiah gave him a curt nod and led Adelaide out of the shop.

They walked down the street a little; then Josiah made an excuse to get away for a moment.

Once Adelaide was safely shopping in another store, he went back to the first shop. He would not be outdone by Adam Bowman! Josiah stepped into the shop, and before he could change his mind, he purchased the gown and bonnet for Adelaide. Adam was nowhere in sight.

⁂

Later that evening, Josiah wondered if he had done the right thing in purchasing the dress and hat. Maybe Adelaide would think it too much. Perhaps she didn't want such a gift from him. Yes, he had gone too far. Such extravagance. But they were out to sea now. He could hardly take them back. Did he have the courage to give them to her?

He needed time to think about it. But where could he store the presents while he thought through the problem?

He might have Adam keep them till the morning. Although it grated him to do it, Josiah knew he could trust Adam with the dress and bonnet. The captain wasn't so sure about anyone else aboard the ship.

Yes, he decided, that's what he'd do. Adam could hold it in his room. Josiah would explain they had little space with Adelaide's things in their rooms. They'd clear something out that night, and Josiah would fetch it in the morning after he decided what to do.

Suddenly, it became very important to Josiah that Adelaide like the gown and matching bonnet. Very important, indeed.

❧

Sticking the last pin in her hair, Adelaide turned with a start when a knock sounded at the door. She knew Josiah wouldn't knock, so she wondered if there was trouble on deck. Quickly, she pulled on her bonnet and went to answer the door. Adelaide opened it and looked up to see Adam holding a box.

"Why, Adam, is everything all right?"

A wide grin stretched across his face. "We caught some more blackfish." Then, as if just remembering the package in his hands, he added, "Oh, here. I thought I'd save you a trip and bring these to you. I hope you have room for them now." Adam stretched his arms out with the packages.

Adelaide puzzled at his comments but took them from him. She didn't know Adam would purchase such a large gift for Esther. In her heart, she was convinced the young man loved her sister. Curiosity got the better of Adelaide. She had to see the gifts. "All right if I look at them?"

Adam's face registered surprise. He shrugged. "I suppose so—"

Just then a voice called behind him. "Captain needs you on deck, sir."

Adam nodded, then turned to Adelaide. He tipped his hat. "See you later, Mrs. Buchanan." With a smile, he turned on his heels and left her staring after him.

Adelaide looked at the boxes, giddy with excitement for her

sister. Quickly, she closed the door behind her. She couldn't get to the sofa fast enough and pull open the packages.

She lifted the lid and peeled back the papers on the smaller box first. "Oh!" She slipped a bonnet from the box. The bonnet she had seen in the dress shop the day before. She removed her bonnet and pulled the new one ever so gently onto her head.

Then with eager fingers, she opened the next box and gasped, staring in disbelief. Adelaide had admired that dress in the shop. Oh, my, to have such a gown! She swallowed hard and lifted the garment ever so gently, allowing its folds to ripple to the ground. Draping it in front of her, she suddenly imagined herself at the most wondrous of balls with Josiah at her side. She curtsied before him, lifting her arms in a dancing gesture, and began to take a few steps in the cramped quarters. So lost was she in her imaginations, she didn't hear the door when it opened.

She turned to see Josiah standing in the entrance, a scowl on his face. "Josiah!" She stopped in her tracks. "Isn't this beautiful? Adam brought it down this morning and—"

"We don't have time for such foolishness, Adelaide. There's blackfish on deck, and you need to get to the cookhouse to prepare it."

All her dreamy notions flew away like a flock of birds, leaving embarrassment behind. What had gotten into her? She had a job to do, and she was behaving foolishly.

"Of course," she answered, humiliation knotting her throat.

Josiah opened his mouth to say something, then seemed to think better of it and turned to go, closing the door behind him.

Large teardrops spilled from her cheeks as Adelaide carefully folded the dress back in place and put the lid on the box. How could she have been so silly? And for Josiah to catch her behaving in such a manner was more than she could bear. For the first time since their trip began, she truly wanted to go home. The sea in all its splendor filled her head with romantic notions. She had to get hold of herself and forget such nonsense. She was on the ship to do a job, and that's precisely what she would do. Nothing more, nothing less. Josiah would get his cook. She would get her life on the sea. That's all each of them wanted, anyway. So what was the problem?

As far as Adelaide was concerned, there was no problem. No problem at all. She brushed aside another tear, ignoring the cries of her heart. Pulling herself up, she washed her face and headed for the door.

Time to cook some blackfish.

ten

Josiah felt cross and worked with a vengeance to get the black-fish on the ship and ready for Adelaide to prepare for lunch. Why had Adam brought that dress to Adelaide? Maybe Josiah hadn't made it clear he wanted to pick it up himself. He gritted his teeth. Now Adelaide thought the gift was from Adam. The worst of it was that she appeared absolutely delighted with the idea.

The whole thing was a big mistake. Marrying Adelaide, bringing her aboard the ship. For what? So he could have a good cook for his crew? Most captains and crews frowned upon allowing a woman on the ship, let alone putting her in charge of the meals. But who could argue with his success? His voyages brought in endless casks brimming with oil and, from the sperm whale he gathered in abundance, spermaceti, the purest of all oils, and ambergris, a substance used in making expensive perfumes, so no one dared oppose his decision to have Adelaide be the cook.

Without question, he had been a fool. What could he do about it now? Approach her with the option of leaving the ship? He knew Adelaide to be a woman of faith, and most likely, she would not consider such a thing. How could he help her escape the dreadful life into which he had entangled her?

❧

"So, what did he get you?" Adam asked Adelaide as he passed her on the way to his cabin.

"Who?"

"Who? Captain, that's who. What was in the boxes?"

She felt her mouth gape and promptly closed it shut. "I–I thought. . ."

83

"What?" His puzzled expression met hers.

"Well, you were getting something for Esther in the dress shop, and I assumed. . ."

Understanding lit his eyes. He whistled and shook his head. "I'm afraid I don't have that kind of money." He shrugged. "I bought her a necklace holding a stone from the island."

Adelaide could hardly contain herself. She could almost kiss Esther's friend. "Oh, how wonderful, Adam. She will love it." She barely noticed him scratching his head as she whisked past him.

Was it possible Josiah had purchased the gown and bonnet for her? Did she dare presume, dare hope? She practically ran up the steps, breathless with excitement. No matter how foolish it seemed, she had to reach him, thank him for his kindness. No wonder he was cross. He realized she had thought the gift was from Adam. But what he didn't know was she thought it was for Esther. Oh, things could get so tangled. But how wonderful she felt.

At last, she found him at the bow of the deck. The crew had just finished with the blackfish, taking it to the cookhouse for her preparation. "Josiah, might I speak with you a moment?"

He threw her a stern look. "I'm rather busy right now, Adelaide." He rinsed his hands in a bucket of water and wiped them with a cloth.

"I know about the dress and bonnet."

His hands stopped midair as he looked at her.

Her voice softened. "I know you bought them for me, and I want to thank you. It is by far the finest garment and bonnet I have ever owned."

"It was foolishness," he said, though his eyes searched her face for more encouragement.

"Foolishness or no, it is beautiful, and I am deeply grateful for your kindness." She touched his arm in a tender gesture, then turned and walked away. Her heart felt giddy with the idea of leaving the mighty sea captain speechless. Besides, she had a new dress and bonnet to try on. Perhaps she would wear it if they went gamming on another ship. She could hardly wait for that to happen. Visiting with other ships brought relief to the lonely days at sea.

❧

Dumbfounded, Josiah stared after Adelaide as she walked across the deck. What had happened, he wasn't sure, but he liked the idea she wanted to keep his gifts. Before he could get too puffed up in his thinking, though, he reminded himself of the look on her face when he had entered their cabin. She was just as happy with the gifts when she thought Adam had purchased them for her. It was the dress and bonnet she wanted, not Josiah.

His clenched jaw relaxed. This was a start, after all. She liked his presents. With any luck, her feelings would eventually grow for him.

❧

The next morning after breakfast, Josiah poked his head in the cabin. "Looks like a whaler close by, Adelaide. The *Majestic*. We shall perhaps have company by evening."

"Wonderful!" Adelaide clapped her hands together. She hoped the captain's wife was on board. She so missed the company of women.

"Good, then. We'll plan on that." With that, he closed the door.

Adelaide could hardly wait. Josiah kept a large tub and a pounding barrel in the house on deck where Adelaide did her laundry for most of the day. Once the starching and ironing was done, she made her way back to the cookhouse for dinner preparations. After dinner, she would clean up for gamming. The excitement of it all carried her through the tiring day.

"I've sent word to the *Majestic*, and they are expecting us within the hour," Josiah said to Adelaide in their room after dinner. "Can you be ready?"

Barely able to contain her joy, she smiled.

"Fine," Josiah said, rising from his chair. "I'll be back to get you in, say, half an hour?"

"Thank you, Josiah."

Adelaide cleared the dishes from the top of her trunk, while Josiah went back on deck. Her heart thumped hard against her ribs. She wasn't sure precisely what one would wear for such an occasion, but she certainly wanted to look her best and knew just the dress and bonnet she would wear. She opened her trunk and pulled out the gifts she had so carefully placed there. She scurried about to get ready. By the time she was finished, she had a few minutes to spare, so she decided to go on deck and meet Josiah.

She could feel the heat rise to her cheeks as she stepped across the deck and felt the admiring gazes of the crew upon her. But when her eyes met Josiah's, her heart took wings.

"Adelaide—" He stopped abruptly.

She looked at him, waiting for him to continue.

He kept staring at her, and she felt a bit awkward with the moment, noticing the crew was watching the two of them. Josiah cleared his throat. "Well, shall we lift you into the gamming chair and lower you to the whaleboat?"

She smiled and nodded. Something told her Josiah was pleased with her appearance, and that thought thrilled her. The crew helped to get Adelaide lowered and settled into the whaleboat, where Josiah joined her. A few of the crewmen accompanied them, while members of the *Majestic*'s crew came from their boat to visit the *Courage*.

Though Adelaide was disappointed there were no women aboard the *Majestic,* she enjoyed the visit with Captain Winifred and Josiah. Captain Winifred presented daguerreotypes of his wife and children for them to look at, which Adelaide greatly enjoyed.

As they departed, Captain Winifred gave them two dozen nice oranges. Also, Adelaide left him with some letters to send home as he was going to port before them. She hoped the letters would reach her family soon.

❧

The weather had been uncomfortably warm, the seas calm, which made for bad whaling. Earlier in the day, they saw whales from the masthead, but before the crew could reach them, the whales had disappeared.

After lunch, Adelaide freshened up in her room, cooling her face with water from the pitcher. She heard another call of a whale sighting. Quickly, she dabbed once more at her face and made her way up the steps to the deck.

Very soon, she saw the sea creature blow and turn flukes, as they called it, or dive toward the ocean bottom. She thought him a formidable creature.

The two mates went off in their boats. Then Josiah went with his boat's crew. The ship received word one of the boats had fastened. The whale continued to spout.

The crews returned in low spirits. Several boats were stoven, and they had to cut from the whale. Adelaide thought they should at least find that whale and make it pay for their boats.

Adelaide watched as the men boarded the ship from the whaleboats. Ebenezer brushed past her mumbling some obscenity, caring nothing about using such language in the presence of a woman. The man infuriated and frightened her. She thought him capable of almost anything. Presently, he walked toward a corner where a few other men were gathered.

What he was up to, she didn't know, but it bothered her. She'd talk to Josiah about it, though she knew Josiah had his own suspicions about Ebenezer Fallon.

Adelaide felt sure they would soon find out more than she wanted to know. She wanted to pray for Ebenezer, but she couldn't push away the feeling of distaste she had for the man. The farther she could stay away from him, the better. He was up to no good. No other way to say it.

Ebenezer Fallon meant trouble.

eleven

Though blackfish and porpoise provided some oil along the way, Josiah wondered at the lack of whales thus far.

Standing at the stern, he looked out to sea. A slight breeze barely lifted the mast. The *Courage* inched its way toward the shores of Rio de la Plata, traveling at three or four knots an hour. Known as good whaling ground, the area raised Josiah's hopes that they would be able to get a few barrels of whale oil.

Breathing in deep of the sea air, Josiah thought about a life on land. How could he ever stop sailing? He shook his head. What would make him ask such a question? A vision of Adelaide popped into his mind. Her delicate features, her gentleness looked so foreign on the likes of a whaling ship. Yet she had her stubborn side—how well he knew. He couldn't help but smile. Deep down, he supposed that's one thing that drew him to her. He liked a woman with a little spirit.

All at once, the breeze kicked up, causing the snap of sails as the wind caught the rigging. The noise temporarily muffled the cry of the crew. Finally, a whaleman approached Josiah. "Captain Buchanan, sir. . ." Panic, coupled with running to the stern, caused his words to squeeze between chokes and great gulps of air. "Your wife—"

Josiah felt his blood run cold. "What is it, man? Out with it!"

The whaleman tried to straighten himself. "Overboard" was all he could manage.

Before the word had left the man's tongue, alarm bolted Josiah halfway across the rolling deck. Men shouted and pointed starboard side. Josiah rushed to a crowd just as a sailor lifted Adelaide onto the ship.

Dripping from their clothes, seawater pooled onto the deck.

The man carefully laid her down. He saw Josiah and stepped aside.

Rushing to Adelaide, Josiah's heart felt like a block of ice. "Adelaide." He turned her, trying to push the water from her lungs. She laid there for what seemed an eternity, then finally coughed out the water and began to breathe. It was then he realized he had been holding his own breath. He took great swigs of air.

Adelaide appeared dazed. Josiah looked up. "Everyone back to your post. She'll be fine." He looked over to the man who had rescued Adelaide.

Josiah lifted his face to him. "I would like to thank you for—" His words froze in his throat. Only then did he realize it was Adam Bowman. The look on Adam's face made Josiah's heart stop. Concern etched the young man's visage, but it was more than that. Perhaps fear of losing the woman they loved gripped them both. A sinking feeling balled in the pit of Josiah's stomach. Before he could say a word to Adam, Adelaide spoke up.

"Who. . . ?"

Josiah swallowed hard and stepped away, pointing toward Adam. "Looks like the first mate came to your rescue."

She reached her hand out to Adam. "Thank you," she managed to say with a weak smile. The look between them said more than Josiah could bear.

In all his days at sea, Josiah had never felt more alone than at that very moment.

&

Josiah took Adelaide back to their room. She put on dry clothes and went to bed. He told her the crew would handle the meals for the rest of the day. She needed to rest. He couldn't make sense out of how she had fallen overboard. Seemed she wasn't quite sure herself; it had all happened so fast.

"You'll be all right, then?"

"I'll be fine."

He turned to go.

"Josiah?"

"Yes?"

"Thank you."

"No need to thank me. I did nothing. I was nowhere around when you needed me. If left to me, you would have drowned." He knew his words sounded harsh, but so be it. Something flickered across her eyes. Most likely sympathy. She felt sorry for him. Sorry that he had failed. They both knew it. The mighty captain couldn't save his own wife. Ah, but the first mate—well, he always stood a stone's throw away, ready to help the lady in distress.

"You're here now."

Her words were barely audible, but they shook him from his self-pity. He grunted. Before he could comment, her eyes closed.

Josiah turned and slipped quietly from their room and latched the door behind him.

Ebenezer met Josiah as he walked up the stairs toward the deck. "Is Mrs. Buchanan all right, Captain?"

Something in Ebenezer's eyes made Josiah want to tell him to mind his own business, but instead he replied, "She's going to be fine."

"Glad to hear it." Ebenezer scratched the whiskers on his chin. "Sure was a good thing Mate Bowman was nearby to save her. Who knows what might have happened." His gaze probed Josiah's eyes, as if he wanted Josiah to read more into his comment. "But then again, guess he's always nearby, isn't he?"

Josiah stared at him.

Ebenezer shrugged. "One can't do without a first mate, that's for sure. Right-hand man, that's what he is. Takes care of business, right down to saving the captain's wife, if need be."

Just then Josiah noticed a few other crewmen nearby listening in. Was this some staged event thought up by this evil man? Did Ebenezer want Josiah to take a swipe at him and give the men an excuse to fight? No, Josiah wouldn't fall for that. He was a captain. He would conduct himself in such a manner.

"Yes, that's right, Ebenezer. A captain can't do without his first mate. I'm thankful to have such a great man for the job." Josiah made himself say the words, though his teeth rebelled at letting them through.

Surprise registered across the crusty sailor's face, and Josiah headed up the stairs, his shoulders relaxing a bit. Once Josiah looked toward the other men, they scattered.

He knew he'd warded off another possible confrontation. He also knew one day soon things would not be so easily smoothed over.

One thought plagued him. Did Ebenezer have something to do with Adelaide's fall? She wasn't sure what had happened. Josiah pounded his right fist into his left palm. If he found out that man had tried to hurt Adelaide. . .

When Adelaide woke up, a black sea sloshed against the hull. A dark sky shadowed the porthole. She couldn't imagine the time. How long had she been in bed? Lifting her head, she raised herself to a sitting position, trying to acclimate herself to what was going on. Her right arm automatically reached down the back of her leg as she remembered hitting it on something just before she had fallen into the water.

She thought back. As she had picked up her washing from a line on deck, a gust of wind had carried a garment from her, and she'd gone to retrieve it. The cloth landed on the railing. She didn't think it that risky to climb up and get it, so she did. The ship suddenly pitched. In her horror, she had tried to balance herself and screamed for help from the nearby sailor. He'd stood motionless and watched her drama unfold. The last thing she saw before being engulfed into the cold, dark sea was the look of pleasure that lit the face of Ebenezer Fallon.

The next thing she knew, she shivered in layers of wet clothes, lying on the hard surface of the ship's deck.

Why hadn't Ebenezer helped her? Could any man be that evil? That inhuman?

Who had helped her? A flash of remembrance came to her. Adam. He stood before her, hair drenched tight to his head, anguish written on his face. Where was Josiah? Oh, yes, he had been there, too. But the look on his face was one of—what? Disgust? Frustration? She couldn't decide.

Then it hit her. She, no doubt, had embarrassed him. After all, she was the captain's wife. What kind of example did she set by falling off the ship? Humiliation washed over her. She had failed poor Josiah. Again.

How could she make it right? How he must regret bringing her with him. Right at this very moment, he probably dreamed of being able to take back those words he had uttered on the shore during the church social.

Her heart ached. How she wanted to make him proud of her. She wanted him to hold her and love her. Be her true husband.

She laid back in her bed, willing herself to forget her responsibilities, her endless chores, her aching heart, everything. Perhaps her dreams would take her to a different life, a life where love prevailed.

છ

Several weeks of snow and hail squalls plagued the *Courage* as it rounded Cape Horn. When the calms came, Adelaide used the time to catch up on her washing, mending, and ironing. She tried to stay out of Josiah's way.

With those chores finished, she wondered what to do with herself. She decided to have one of the men kill a hog from their livestock so she could make sausage meat. Once the killing was done, Adelaide prepared the meat and filled eight good-sized bags.

Her back ached and her body felt sore from her recent chores. She made her way to their cabin. Josiah caught her on deck.

"There's a ship close by, Adelaide. Maybe we can visit with them tonight."

Though she felt tired, she could hardly wait to enjoy the company of the captain and hopefully his wife. "I'd like that."

"Good. You rest for a while, and I'll let you know when we're close enough."

She nodded and decided to do that very thing.

The next couple of nights, Adelaide and Josiah enjoyed gamming with the *Victory's* captain and wife, sharing meals together and talking of life on the seas.

A few days later, they parted company, each heading in different directions with little hope of reconnecting in the near future.

Adelaide hated to see them leave. The distance between Josiah and her had greatly lengthened since her dip in the ocean. She knew without a doubt she had failed him. On the one hand, shame filled her for her stupidity in falling off the ship, but anger also filled her because he had so harshly judged her. People made mistakes. She didn't know perfection was a qualifying factor to be Mrs. Josiah Buchanan.

No doubt Catherine Buchanan had been perfect in every way. Not a clumsy fool. Adelaide sat on her chair in their room and pulled a needle through the material a little too fast. She poked her finger. "Oh!" She pulled her hand free and instinctively sucked on her finger. The pinprick did little to encourage her spirits.

She threw the material down and paced the tiny room. "Why should I feel bad? It's not as though I planned to fall." She took three steps, turned, and headed in the opposite direction. "It's not as though he never made a mistake," she said, shaking her hands in the air—though it made her mad to know she couldn't think offhand of any mistakes he had made.

The more she thought about it, the angrier she became. Who did he think he was, bringing her on this dirty ship to feed a crew of burly seamen? And to have the nerve to pretend he was doing her a favor at that! Oh, sure she had wanted to sail the seas, but like this? He had played on her emotions, that's what. She paced some more, each new footstep hitting the plank harder than the last.

Her chin pointed heavenward. Well, she needn't feel embarrassed. So she had fallen. Wouldn't be the first time someone had fallen into the ocean and most certainly wouldn't be the last. She would not let him make her feel stupid or small. From what she knew of other captain's wives, she felt herself just as qualified.

Oh, the more she thought about the whole affair, the angrier she got. She could hardly wait for Josiah to come to their cabin. She'd let him know in no uncertain terms she was just as good a captain's wife as any of the other wives. Including his precious Catherine. And furthermore, if he didn't like how she conducted herself, why, he could let her off at the next port and she'd get herself home somehow. She was tired of feeling used and unappreciated.

Self-pity engulfed her, and she didn't care. She was tired and spent. Did the men appreciate all her hard work? Clearly, Josiah did not. She could have been a crewman for all he cared. He noticed nothing about her except her cooking. Though she knew that wasn't entirely true in recent days, she refused to go soft.

A voice went off inside her head. *Isn't that what the agreement was? You would cook and get to sail the seas.* Adelaide kicked her boot across the floor. "I hate the agreement. I never wanted that agreement. I wanted. . .Josiah."

Before the tears could flood her eyes, their door swung open. A flushed Josiah stood at the entrance. "Adelaide." He stopped, licked his lips, and looked at her again. "I don't feel so—"

His words were cut short as his body hit the floor in a crumpled heap.

twelve

"We have to stop at Pequeno Island, Adam." Adelaide wrenched her hands together. "Josiah is sick. Very sick. I think he contracted something from the last ship with which we made contact."

Adam looked at her thoughtfully. "Have you been able to discuss this with Josiah?" Adam's eyes held worry.

Adelaide shook her head. "He's feverish, doesn't have a clear thought. We will get to help."

"How long will we need to be at Pequeno?"

"However long it takes Josiah to get well," she said with a voice that let him know he dare not challenge her.

"The men won't like it."

"Doesn't matter. It's what we're going to do." She surprised herself at the authority in her voice.

"All right, Adelaide. We'll stop. Should get there tomorrow by nightfall."

Adelaide took a deep breath. "Thank you." She walked away and immediately made a mental note of the things she would do once they reached port.

The next night after the ship anchored, Adelaide and Adam made their way into town in search of someone to help them. Once they located a doctor, he quickly followed them and came on board the ship.

Adelaide took him to their room and sat in the corner while the stranger went to work. He pulled open his bag, lifting various instruments with which to poke, prod, and stick her husband.

Round spectacles circled his beady eyes, giving him a doctorly appearance. He said very little as he worked with his patient. Josiah lay very still. The fever had subsided, but his skin looked pale as muslin. Fear held Adelaide's breath in place. She was afraid to move until the doctor spoke, letting her know Josiah's condition.

Before long, the doctor began to stuff his things back into the bag; then he stood to look at her.

"Can't say what it is for sure, but most likely the tropical fever that's been going around. I've seen more than one ship come in of late with men groaning of the fever. He'll be all right, but it will take several days to work it out of his system. Makes a fellow weak, though. Most important thing is that he has to rest. If he doesn't rest, it can go into something far worse, so you have to keep him still no matter what. Hopefully, no one else will get it."

Her mind raced for answers. How could she keep a busy sea captain down? Especially one with a restless crew?

"How long?"

"Week, two weeks. Depends." The man shrugged. "I don't know your husband's condition before the fever. That makes a difference on the recuperation period." He walked toward the door. "Keep him sponged off with cool water. I've left you some medicine packets," he added, pointing toward the table. "Just to make sure it is the fever, you'd better not leave for a couple of days. I'll be back and check on him then."

Before she could say another word, he was out the door. Adelaide sighed. She stood in place, trying to decide which way to turn next. First, she would inform the crew. But how could she leave Josiah, even if only for a short time? What if he needed her? What if he woke up delirious? She bit her lip. Seemed she could always think better that way.

Fortunately, she didn't have to think too long. Another knock sounded at the door.

"Yes?"

"Adelaide—I mean, Mrs. Buchanan?"

Adelaide recognized Adam's voice and opened the door.

"Come in, Adam."

He stepped in and took off his hat. "How's he doing?"

Adelaide explained what the doctor had told her. Adam looked worried. "What is it?"

He shook his head as he heard her explanation. "The crew is mighty restless. I shouldn't say it, but I don't trust Ebenezer Fallon."

She blew out a sigh of understanding. "It's all right. We feel the same way." She turned a worried look to Josiah. "Let's give him a couple of days and see how he does. Maybe by then, Josiah can tell me how he wants to proceed." She turned back to Adam. "We must stay near help for a couple of days to get through the worst of it. I will not risk his life, not even for the entire ship."

Adam nodded. "I'll try to keep them calm. We'll get through this. I'll be praying."

"Thank you, Adam."

He closed the door behind him, and Adelaide stood staring. She hadn't had a chance to think about praying until now. Quietly, she eased onto her knees beside her trunk.

She didn't know how long she had prayed, but sometime later, with aching legs, she rose to her feet, her face wet with tears, but her heart feeling much lighter. She knew God had heard her prayer and would help them through. Just how, she didn't know, but she knew they were not alone.

The next morning, Adelaide awoke as Josiah was groaning and speaking unintelligible words. She got up and went to him. His face burned with fever. A rush of alarm spread through her. The doctor said he should be getting better with rest. What had happened? Maybe it was more than what the doctor had suspected.

She quickly ran to the pitcher of water, grabbed a rag, and went to Josiah. She bathed his face over and over until the cloth itself felt warm from his body heat. Bringing a cup to his lips, she tried to get him to drink, but he couldn't. She didn't know where the doctor lived, and it was too early for him to be in his office. A glance at her timepiece told her it was almost four o'clock.

What could she do? She hurried to the pitcher, dipped the cloth, wrung it out, then went back to his bed and continued to bathe him.

"Catherine."

Adelaide's hand froze midair. She held her breath and waited for him to say more.

"Why?" Josiah's head turned back and forth, back and forth. Agonizing groans escaped him.

Adelaide shook his arms to free him from his painful memories. "Josiah, it's Adelaide. Josiah." He never opened his eyes, but his head stopped turning, and his groans grew silent.

When his fever had somewhat subsided, Adelaide walked over, exhausted, to her own bed. The light of day had dawned, and she could hear the sleepy town rising to greet it. She collapsed in her blankets with one agonizing thought. Josiah still loved Catherine.

ʾ

Five days later, Josiah woke up with a start. What had happened? His eyes adjusted to the morning light that filtered in through the porthole. The ship didn't feel right. Must be in another calm. Why was he in bed? Were they in port? If so, who had given the orders to pull into port? He rubbed his head. It hurt. Questions rushed through his mind, but he couldn't work through the tangled maze. He had to get up. He attempted to lift himself from the bed, but his elbows were too weak. He fell back. Something stirred in Adelaide's bed. She lay sleeping and hadn't drawn the curtain between them.

Obviously, she wanted to watch him. Why? He saw the chair near his bed, the rag, the pitcher of water. The medicine. Had he been sick? The throbbing in his head and the weakness in his limbs answered his question.

He lay still, looking at Adelaide. She was so different from

Catherine. His first wife would never have bothered with him in his sickness. She left him. Her thoughts were selfish and cruel. While Adelaide cared so generously for others—even him—when he least deserved it.

Just like God.

Where did that thought come from? The only sounds he heard were the thoughts rushing through his mind. Adelaide did love God, and it showed. A God of whom he knew very little. Did he want to know more? What about the people at church who talked about him and about Catherine's rejection? What about his pain at sea—did God care about that? Why did He let her go? Why did God let Catherine hurt him that way?

He wanted to shake his head and make all the thoughts go away, but his head hurt too much. Was he going to die? What if what they said about God and eternity were true? Was he ready to meet his Maker?

Fear gripped his heart. He knew he wasn't ready. Being ready required forgiveness. And God could not forgive Josiah until Josiah forgave Catherine and the church people who had hurt him. He knew that much about the gospel message.

He didn't want to make a deathbed confession. His integrity would not allow it. Would he merely use God to make it to heaven? No, he had to mean it regardless of whether he lived or died, and Josiah wasn't sure he could forgive Catherine. Ever.

"Josiah!" Adelaide scrambled from her covers and rushed to him. "Oh, Josiah, you're awake." Tears flooded down her cheeks.

Her concern touched him deeply.

She looked as though she would throw herself over him in one swoop, but her steps came to a sudden halt. Josiah managed a half smile, which she matched.

Adelaide settled herself into the chair beside the bed and told him what had transpired in the last five days. He thought on what she said, trying to sort out what to do from here.

Someone knocked on the door.

Adelaide stood. "Yes, who is it?"

"Dr. Walters."

Adelaide looked at Josiah, then opened the door.

Dr. Walters walked in, weariness on his face. "Is he any better?" His expression told her he had little hope.

"See for yourself," Adelaide said with a smile, motioning toward the bed.

Dr. Walters let out a laugh. "Well, if you aren't a sight for sore eyes." The doctor expertly went through his routine and checked Josiah out. When the exam was over, he announced the good news that Josiah could sail the next day if he so chose, but he'd still need to take it somewhat easy in the days ahead.

Following Josiah's instructions, Adelaide told Adam they would be setting sail the next morning at dawn. The crew should be ready to go.

Adelaide purchased a few things for dinner and brought them to their room. The pleasant scent of spices, meat, and potatoes made Adelaide's stomach growl. Only then did she realize how little she had been eating.

Though Josiah could eat very little, he tried a few bites. He stirred the potatoes on his plate. "Thank you for taking care of me."

Adelaide looked up and smiled. "You'd have done the same for me."

"Catherine would never have done that."

Adelaide dropped her fork. She wasn't accustomed to him bringing up his first wife's name.

"She hurt me, you know."

"I know." Adelaide felt his pain. "I'm sorry, Josiah."

He shrugged. "I don't know why I let it bother me so much over the last couple of years. I suppose it was pride. I just hadn't expected her to do that."

Adelaide listened, never saying a word lest he stop.

"I've been a fool." He ran his fingers through his hair. He stopped and looked at her. "I want to know God the way you do, Addie."

Warmth rushed clear through her.

"I don't understand why she did what she did, but I don't want it to keep me from God."

"People make choices, Josiah. Those choices affect others. Good or bad. Catherine's choice affected you. The good news is that God's choice to love sinners, shown through the death of His Son on a cross, can change a life that trusts in Him. You don't have to let Catherine's choice cause you to make the wrong choice about God. He is there for you. Always has been. Always will be."

Josiah nodded.

"The church folks you told me about probably just didn't know what to say. Sometimes folks feel it's better to say nothing than to say the wrong thing."

He nodded. "You're right. I've allowed my own imaginings to run away with me. I want to make the right choice now, Addie. Will you pray with me?"

Tears plopped on her dress, and she nodded. She led him in a prayer of confession and repentance to God.

Once they had finished praying, Adelaide wiped her tears and looked at Josiah. She placed her hand on his. "You know, Josiah, the prayer is only the beginning. The joy comes from having a continuing walk with Christ. Spending time with Him through His Word, allowing Him to lead you through life. It's an incredible journey."

He wiped his face, smiled, and nodded. "That's what I want—a changed life."

Adelaide smiled while her spirit soared. Though their situation hadn't changed, she felt certain their future would never be the same.

thirteen

Adelaide stepped up on deck to get some fresh air. Josiah was feeling much better, though his strength still waned. The sickness allowed him to get up only a few hours each day; then he headed back to bed. The admission of weakness didn't come easily for the rugged sea captain. Adelaide knew he would never go to bed unless forced to do so.

She took a deep breath. At least no one else got the sickness, and for that they could all be thankful. Still, she knew the extra days in port did little to help the morale of the crew.

Footsteps sounded just behind her. "Mrs. Buchanan?"

Adelaide turned to face Adam. She smiled. "How are you?"

His expression turned sober. "Not good." He looked at his feet. "I'm sorry to bother you with this, but, well, with the captain down, I don't know what else to do."

"What is it, Adam?"

"It's the men. Ebenezer's got 'em stirred up. Convinced them the whales are in the Gulf of Alaska, and the captain is wasting their time if he heads only as far as the Sandwich Islands."

She stared at Adam, biting her lip. "If only we could catch another whale."

"I fear a mutiny, Adelaide," he whispered. "I mean, Mrs. Buchanan."

She waved away his formalities, her mind already trying to figure out how to handle the situation. "I'll see what I can do. Thanks for your help."

He nodded, a worried look still on his face.

"Keep praying," she told him. With that, Adelaide turned and walked toward the cookhouse to prepare lunch.

Working hard on the meal, Adelaide prepared a feast of

ham, Irish potatoes, cabbage, string beans, and goat's milk for the crew, hoping to calm them down through their stomachs. Once her work was finished, she left the cookhouse and carried a meal for her and Josiah to their room.

Adelaide felt Josiah's gaze on her when they settled into their chairs.

"You want to tell me about it?"

She flipped out her napkin and looked up in feigned surprise. "What do you mean?"

His hand swept across the table. "This meal tells me something's wrong. This is not our normal fare for lunch."

Of course he would pick up on that. How silly of her. Adelaide sighed. "The men are restless, Josiah. It's Ebenezer. I believe he's trying to convince them the whales are in the gulf and you're wrong to go only as far as the islands. Adam told me, though we have no real proof, unfortunately."

Josiah rubbed his chin thoughtfully. "I see."

Adelaide said little more, knowing Josiah was working out the issue in his mind. They finished the meal in silence.

Before Adelaide could clear the table, Josiah grabbed her hand. "Join me in prayer, Adelaide. We need direction."

How those words thrilled her heart! The two of them prayed for discernment. Afterward, the exercise of prayer seemed to have tired Josiah. "I'm afraid I'll have to deal with it when my strength returns." He looked at Adelaide apologetically and climbed back in bed.

Adelaide still feared for him. Though the doctor had told her the danger was over, she had never seen him so frail.

She stood and gathered the things she wanted to take back to the cookhouse. She needed to clean up after the crew. First, she would clean the dishes; then she would go.

Once the dishes were cleaned, Adelaide stepped from the cabin to make her way to the cookhouse. She heard a commotion from the forecastle. Though a woman should never go near the men's quarters, she edged her way closer in hopes of hearing what was going on. She stopped short when she saw Josiah's form standing in the shadows. She could hear the men grumbling among themselves, Ebenezer's voice urging them on. Then out of the rumble, she heard Adam's voice.

"Now look here. Captain Buchanan has been good to us. He feeds us far better than any other whaling ship on these waters, and you know it. He sees to it we stop in port when we need a change. He's been entirely fair in his dealings with us. Now all of a sudden you think he's trying to cheat us. Why?"

Adam's voice held more authority than Adelaide had ever heard before. She felt proud of him for standing up for Josiah.

"I say this sickness is turning him yellow," Ebenezer called out. "He's weak and afraid to take on a whale now. Too bad for him. We still have to make money with or without him. I say we go to the gulf!" Ebenezer's voice was raised now, exciting the men to action.

Adelaide gasped as she watched Josiah step through the shadows, bringing the room to instant silence.

Josiah raised his arms. "I understand your concerns. No one wants to waste time. We're all trying to make a living here." He turned his unrelenting gaze on Ebenezer. "I'm not trying to make you suffer because of my illness." Josiah measured his words evenly, as if carefully considering what to say next. "In talking with the other captains along our journey, I've been told the weather will be severe this year in the gulf. It didn't seem prudent to risk being trapped by the ice. We've heard of more than one incident where ships have been trapped and eventually destroyed by the icebergs—"

Ebenezer waved his hand. "Yellow, like I said. We ain't afraid of no ice!" His voice thundered with rebellion. He turned to the men. "You gonna let him scare you into missing an opportunity of a lifetime? I'm telling you, the whales are there!"

Adelaide heard a faint sound on deck. She turned. The masthead. The sound came from the masthead. She slipped up the stairs.

"There she blows!" the seaman cried.

Excitement surged through her. She ran back toward the forecastle as fast as her legs could carry her. "A whale. We have our whale!" she cried. The men scattered as fast as the words left her lips.

Relief washed over Adelaide. Josiah looked at her and smiled. They would catch this whale.

God had heard their prayer.

❧

A squall kicked up, making it difficult for the men to fasten the two whales. The ship reeled to and fro like a drunken man. Adelaide could not bear to watch the whaleboats being tossed about from wave to wave.

Her fear subsided when the crew returned with somewhat small, though in Adelaide's view impressive, whales.

The crew immediately set to cutting in and boiling, working day and night. Adelaide watched the pilot fish, skipjack, and albacore that followed the ship for the refuse of the whale that was thrown overboard. The air seemed black with the hundreds of storm petrels that hovered just over the surface of the water. The stench and sight, though still gruesome and overpowering, did not make Adelaide sick like before. She felt proud she was growing accustomed to the life on a whaling ship.

The next morning, Adelaide prepared albacore for breakfast. The crew finally stowed away sixty barrels of oil from the blubber and commenced to salting down some albacore for trade at the islands.

They caught more pilot fish. Adelaide thought them a pretty fish, about the size of a trout, blue with black stripes, and considered very nice eating. She decided to prepare the pilot fish for dinner.

Just after lunch, Josiah asked Adelaide to summon Adam Bowman into their quarters. She knew Josiah didn't care much for Adam, though she couldn't understand why. Josiah seemed to have taken a dislike to Adam from day one. Not that any of it should concern her. Josiah was the captain. Be that as it may, Adam was her friend, and she hoped the two men could settle their differences.

Once back in their room, Adelaide tidied the area while Josiah relaxed on his bed. A knock sounded at the door, and Adelaide opened it to allow Adam entrance.

He pulled off his cap. "Ma'am." He turned to Josiah. "Captain? You wanted to see me?"

Josiah raised himself from the bed and walked over to the table. "Have a seat, Bowman."

Adam complied.

"Would you like me to leave, Josiah?" Adelaide asked.

"No, I'd like you to stay."

Not knowing what to do with herself, Adelaide sorted through her clothes just to keep her hands busy.

"First off, I want to apologize to you," Josiah began.

Adelaide's fingers stopped moving through the cloth. She couldn't imagine what Josiah would say next.

"I've been utterly unfair to you from the start."

Adelaide dared a glance at Adam and thought his expression priceless. He looked as though he'd swallowed a fish whole. She stifled a chuckle.

"I allowed foolish thinking to get in the way of good sense."

Though Adelaide hadn't a clue what he meant, and she could see confusion on Adam's face as well, she was proud of Josiah for taking this hard step.

Josiah swallowed hard. "I never did properly thank you for rescuing Adelaide from the water that day, and I want to thank you for helping me with the men before a mutiny erupted. You've been a top-rate officer, and I'm beholden to you."

Adam blushed. "Wouldn't Esther be proud?" Adelaide said with a smile.

Josiah turned to look at Adelaide. "Esther?"

"Well, yes. Didn't you know Adam was sweet on my sister?"

Adam fingered the cap in his hands. "I'd say it was more than that, Mrs. Buchanan. I want her to be my wife—if she'll have me."

Adelaide saw the surprise on Josiah's face and laughed. "You mean you didn't know?"

Josiah shook his head. "No idea."

Adelaide watched as a pleasant countenance fell upon Josiah. No doubt about it, things were changing for them.

&

Adelaide fried the pilot fish for dinner and served the remainder for breakfast the next morning. Josiah didn't much care for the fish, so he ate some eggs. About ten minutes after their breakfast, Adelaide's face began to burn, and her head ached. A glance in the looking glass made her gasp. Her face was as red as a lobster all over: chin, forehead, ears, and neck.

Adelaide got into her bed and prayed Josiah would come back and check on her. At this rate, she would not be able to prepare lunch.

About midmorning, Josiah stepped into their room, took one look at her, and made a face. "I didn't know what was wrong with the crew until I looked at you. Now I know that you've all been poisoned by eating the fish that we kept overnight."

"Oh, dear, Josiah. I'm so sorry."

He shrugged. "You didn't know. Everyone will be fine by tomorrow. But you all will feel pretty nasty for the remainder of the day. I don't think there's much need to worry about the lunch and dinner. Most of the crew ate the fish."

She nodded.

A smile tugged at his lips. "You are a sight for sore eyes," he teased.

Adelaide grabbed her head. "Just wait, Captain Buchanan, I'll get you for this." She managed a smile, then a groan.

"Rest well, Mrs. Buchanan," he said, slipping out the door.

fourteen

Adelaide and the crew felt better by the next day. With the crew's renewed strength came restlessness for more whales. Long days of inactivity did little good for them. The head winds and calms added to a great deal of rough weather didn't help matters. The calms caused the ship to move slowly, and Ebenezer continued to let them know there was little time to lose.

Adelaide prayed they'd catch another whale soon, before Ebenezer could cause more trouble.

One of the whalemen grew sick with pneumonia. Josiah said if the man didn't get better soon, they'd have to leave him at the islands. The forecastle offered few conveniences for sickness. Adelaide worried the illness would overtake some others.

While sitting in her room mending clothes, Adelaide thought of the last months at sea. Her head had been so full of romantic notions. Pa had told her what she wanted to hear. He'd left out the bad parts. She smiled and let out a sigh. So like Pa. How she missed him.

Though she still loved the sea, Adelaide had learned much from her short time aboard the *Courage*. It was a hard life. Sickness, disgruntled men, accidents, loneliness—they all plagued the seafaring man. An ache squeezed her heart as she thought of Ma and Esther. Adelaide wondered about their health. Did Ma have enough help with only Esther there? Adelaide breathed deeply and closed her eyes. What was done was done, and she couldn't go back and change things now. She had to make the best of it. And so she would.

Josiah burst through the door, quite out of breath. "Another whale, Addie." He grabbed something from the room and left.

She lifted her gaze heavenward. "Thank You." As long as the whales appeared, Ebenezer couldn't stir up the crew. She said a prayer for the men, then rushed to the deck.

Adelaide held tightly to the ship's rail, watching the wind toss about the whaleboats. Strong waves lifted them to great lengths, then dropped them without mercy. The men continued to row vigorously. In the distance, the whale spouted his presence, almost in a teasing fashion. Adelaide's stomach spasmed from the constant motion. The angry seas pelted hard against the ship, biting into her skin. She fought against worry.

After the boats were a distance out, Adelaide decided to go to the cookhouse and work on dinner. Before she turned, someone yelled, "Stoven boat."

Adelaide jerked around and looked back out to sea. Her heart caught in her throat. She watched as the men in the other whaleboats paddled hard and fast to get to the men tossed from their boat. She pulled a handkerchief from her dress pocket and twisted it in her hands. Her lips uttered another prayer. Where was Josiah?

She strained her neck to get a glimpse, desperately trying to find Josiah in the crowd. The ship tossed about, and water formed a mist across her eyes, making it impossible to recognize the men in the distance. She finally gave up and went downstairs to nurse her queasy stomach.

By the time the men came back, Adelaide had returned to the deck, though still feeling a little out of sorts. As the men climbed aboard, she saw that they had fastened the whale, though their countenance showed no trace of excitement. Something was wrong, but she didn't know what.

Fear sliced through her until Josiah came into view. She breathed a sigh of relief. He walked over to her. "We've lost a man, Adelaide."

She gasped. "Oh, Josiah, no." Her eyes searched his face. "Who was it?"

"Ebenezer Fallon."

A pain shot through her. "Not Ebenezer. He wasn't ready to meet the Lord, Josiah." She lifted tears to him.

"I know." Josiah reached up and tenderly brushed the tears from her face. Someone called to him for assistance. "Be right there." He turned back to Adelaide.

"How did it happen?"

"He was drunk. Couldn't handle himself with a stoven boat."

"Once the oil is stowed, are you planning a service for Ebenezer?"

Josiah nodded, then turned and walked away.

Adelaide walked near the vicinity of the whale and stood in awe. She could never have imagined such a sight. Her pa had told her a right whale's massive head contained fifteen hundred pounds of bone. Looking at it now, she believed him. The display before her was both gruesome and spectacular.

The crew quickly commenced to cutting and boiling. They worked tirelessly stowing the 155 barrels of oil just before another gale stirred up, obliging them to put out the fires and stop the tryworks. The weather would not permit them to gather on the deck. Josiah decided the service for Ebenezer would be put off till after they went to port.

Following their hard work, a dead calm plagued them. Miserable whaling weather. The *Courage* pulled into the nearest port for trading. The customhouse officer came on board, and shortly after, the ship anchored.

Knowing the stop was strictly for business, Adelaide stayed on board.

Once Josiah returned, he told her they had received $1.50 per pound for the whalebone. An unheard-of price.

"I suppose we have the ladies, with all their hoops and corsets, to thank for such a fine price," Josiah teased.

Adelaide's face grew warm. "May the fashion long continue," she said with a smile.

❧

With the ship back on course, Josiah made arrangements for the crew to meet on deck in the evening for Ebenezer's service.

Josiah spoke of the vastness of the heavenly Father's creative power. With a sweep of his arms, he talked of the majesty and dangers of the seas and the surety of eternity.

Genuinely mourning for Ebenezer's soul, Josiah spoke of forgiveness. Who knew what Ebenezer's life had been like? Josiah explained to the crew someone had once told him life was full of choices. He turned to Adelaide and smiled, then continued with his speech. "Our choices tangle together with the choices of other people, each affecting the other." He spoke words of comfort and finally ended the service with a prayer for all who were still living, that they might learn to make the right choices.

The crew dispersed. A whaleman came over to Josiah. He fidgeted with the cap in his hands. "After what he did to you and your wife, I don't know how you could forgive him."

"After all that God has forgiven us, can we do any less?"

The man scratched his head.

"I'm not saying it's easy to forgive people who wrong you, only that there's no peace without it."

"I let him get me stirred up." The man looked down at the deck. "I'm sorry, sir."

"People can be persuasive. Let it be a lesson to you to stand strong next time."

The sailor stopped fidgeting with his cap and looked at Josiah with thankful eyes. "I'm proud to serve with you, sir."

He smiled. "And we're proud to have you. My prayers are with you."

The man's eyes grew wide. "I'm obliged." He turned and walked away.

Josiah knew God was working in the hearts of the crew. He prayed that through this misfortune, the men would come to know the Lord.

Over the next several weeks, the *Courage* made good headway. The catch of another large whale kept the crew busy.

Once the deck was scrubbed back to normal, Adelaide enjoyed walking on board and watching the clouds that hovered overhead. The weather, calm and warm, provided the perfect setting for Adelaide as she pulled her chair out on the deck. With her journal in hand, she made her entry: *March 4.* Making it a point to stay current with the news every chance she got, Adelaide remembered having read in a newspaper that on this very day the newly elected president, James Buchanan, would take his seat in the presidential chair. She wondered if Josiah could be distantly related to the new president.

Life seemed so different on the seas than on land. She thought it a wonder they were fortunate enough to hear who had won the election at all when they were so far from home.

"Enjoying yourself?" Josiah's voice warmed her more than the sun.

"Uh-huh." She closed her journal and looked at him. They were growing closer, but would they ever be man and wife? She dreamed of the day. She hoped it would happen. One day.

"Walk with me to the rail?" He extended his hand to her. Adelaide reached for it and rose from her chair. Together they walked to the railing and looked out to sea.

"We've been on our journey over three months now." His gaze fixed on the waters, he seemed to be speaking to no one in particular. He hesitated as if afraid to say the next words. Turning to her, he asked, "Are you happy, Adelaide?" His eyes searched hers.

She looked him full in the face and said with certainty, "I'm very happy, Josiah."

Lost in the moment, neither one pulled away. Josiah looked for all he was worth as though he wanted to kiss her. Wanting him to desperately, yet not wanting to create a spectacle in front of the crew, Adelaide blinked, bringing both of them to their senses.

Josiah cleared his throat. "Good," he said matter-of-factly. He looked back toward the sea. "We should arrive on Akaroa Island sometime tomorrow afternoon. Hope to stay about a week, do some trading, give the men a chance to relax, buy more supplies."

Adelaide smiled, excited at the thought of being on land awhile. "We're still a ways south of New Zealand, right?"

"Right," he answered with a smile.

She smiled back, knowing he understood her struggle with directions.

"I'll let you get back to your journal," he said. Once more he turned to her and brushed a strand of hair from her cheek. He smiled, then walked away, leaving her cheek burning where his finger had been.

❧

The following morning, Adelaide prepared for fishing. Josiah helped her place a piece of white cloth onto a hook and instructed her to bob it up and down to make it look like a flying fish. By morning's end, she felt a bit puffed up with pride for having caught several large fish. Josiah seemed proud of her and suggested she cook her catch for lunch, which she immediately set out to do.

By early afternoon, the ship had arrived at the shores of Akaroa Island. The wharf bustled with activity when the *Courage* finally anchored. Ships lined the port. Crewmen spilled onto the shores, anxious to explore the island. Some stayed behind and worked busily on ship repairs. Adelaide thought the sights spectacular. As soon as they anchored, the customhouse officer came on board with a boat's crew of natives. Josiah followed them for the purpose of obtaining a boarding place while on shore.

Within a couple hours, Adelaide and Josiah were in the boat on their way to the house of Paul and Ruth Burks. Longing for the company of another woman, Adelaide was disappointed the Burks were traveling abroad and would not be there. Still, she could hardly wait to get settled into a real home.

Upon arrival, the straw cottage surprised her. Exotic trees and flowers surrounded it, making it appear every bit the island home. Its backyard faced the shoreline.

The cook and two women who took care of the house greeted Adelaide and Josiah and showed them around.

The house consisted of four rooms: a sitting room, two bedrooms, and a dining room. The sitting room extended the whole length of the house with a door opening at either end. Crimson and white drapery adorned four windows. Chinese chairs, lounges, and a sofa provided comfortable and decorative seating. Other furnishings included a secretary and library and center and side tables, while bright paintings and engravings hugged the walls, giving the room a homey feel.

"Do you like it?" Josiah whispered when no one was around.

"Very much."

"Good."

A knock sounded at the door. Josiah opened it. An islander stood in the entrance. "Captain Buchanan?"

"Yes?"

"You have an urgent letter, sir," the young man said in polished English as he handed Josiah an envelope.

Fear gripped Adelaide as she worried that it might be bad news from home.

Josiah thanked the man and worked quickly to open the envelope. Adelaide watched as he stared at the paper, all color draining from his face. "What is it, Josiah?"

He turned a glazed look her way. Staring for a moment, he finally said, "It's not about your family. I can't talk about it now." With envelope in hand, Josiah pushed through the doors, leaving a speechless Adelaide behind.

fifteen

Josiah walked up one street, then another. Though the fever had left him weaker than it had found him, he continued to walk. He lifted the crumpled envelope in his hands time and again. Funny how a letter could change your life forever.

A child. He had a child. He paced with only a cursory glance at the colorful birds that swooped down upon the bright green foliage enhancing the land. His thoughts held him captive. What would he do with a child? He knew nothing of raising one. His hand absently raked through his hair. Suddenly, his footsteps came to an abrupt halt.

Adelaide.

He had asked her to be his cook. But a mother? Just when things were growing between them, would he lose her, too?

Why hadn't Catherine told him she was pregnant? Did she despise him so much she would withhold his own child from him? Had he known her so little?

The Bayview Orphanage had written that Catherine had died in childbirth. Though Catherine's mother raised the child for a short time, poverty and ill health had forced her to take the child to the orphanage. The orphanage had been searching for Josiah over the past two years, hoping to unite him with his daughter.

His daughter.

He kicked a stone in his path. Not that he wasn't thankful for a child, but to gain one in this way? He couldn't help but feel somewhat responsible for Catherine's death. She had made wrong choices, true, but he hadn't exactly been the best husband. What kind of father would he be?

While some people took their children aboard whaling

ships, he wasn't sure he could do that. Life was hard on the seas. Did he want his daughter raised around a band of rough crewmen?

A more troubling thought nagged at him. Could he continue whaling? The last few whale catches had tired him beyond belief. He thought once he got over his illness, he would be good as new. Yet his former strength eluded him. He questioned his ability to continue. So many questions, so many decisions to make.

What do I do, Lord? Josiah felt at the end of himself. This was something he couldn't fix. After hours of thinking, he decided he'd head back to the cottage. Most likely, Adelaide was in a state of confusion over his actions. How should he break the news to her?

"Yes, Adelaide, you're about to become a mother." He groaned. How could things get any worse? Raw emotion seared through him, with shame following close behind.

It's not that he didn't love children. Thoughts of having a child softened him. A faceless girl played before his mind. A toddler.

Being methodical by nature, he'd take it one step at a time. What else could he do?

The first step was to tell Adelaide the news. Her reaction would determine the next.

જા

Adelaide couldn't imagine what news Josiah had received. Whatever its content, it couldn't be good. Other than when he was sick, she had never seen him so pale. She wanted to help him, but how could she since she didn't know what the problem was?

Of course, he didn't share the problem with her. True, they had grown closer, but they weren't truly husband and wife—yet.

She sat on a chair in the backyard, drinking in the liquid blue of the sky, the smell of the sea, the lush greenery. What would her friends back home say if they could see her now? If only she could take these sights home with her to share. Even then, she couldn't imagine adequately describing the place to them. If only Ma and Esther could be with her now.

If Ma were here, she'd know what to do for Josiah. Visions of long talks with Ma on the porch filled Adelaide's mind. "Oh, God, show me how to help him. Give me the strength to hear his news and help him through it."

❧

Josiah rehearsed the words in his mind all the way back to the cottage. He couldn't worry about it. The words had to be said, and they would deal with the situation accordingly. After all, this little girl was his flesh and blood. He would not neglect her. Who knew what her life had been up to now?

Taking the last step up to their temporary home, Josiah drew in a ragged breath before opening the door. He stepped inside.

"Adelaide?" He went from room to room in search of her. With a quick glance out the window, he saw her sitting in the backyard. His heart stirred. He loved her. No denying it. Adelaide was an understanding woman, full of compassion. She'd stand by him. Why did he worry?

He pushed through the door and stepped out into the backyard. Upon seeing him, Adelaide rose from her chair. Her questioning eyes made him want to wrap her in his arms. The unspoken words kept them apart.

"I need to talk to you."

She nodded.

Josiah cleared his throat. He reached into his pocket and pulled out the crumpled envelope. He stared at it a moment. "This letter holds some disturbing news, I'm afraid." Oh, how could he tell her this? How would she react? He decided to go for the lighthearted approach. "It seems. . ." He stared at his boots, not daring to look at her. "It seems that I'm a father." He glanced up in time to see her teeter in place. His eyes fixed on her. She said nothing. "Addie? Are you all right?"

She looked as though cold water had been doused in her face. "A father?"

Her eyes looked all liquid and brown. He wanted to hold her, tell her things would work out, plead with her to understand. "Seems Catherine was with child when I set sail." He stared across the waters. "I never knew." The words lifted softly out to sea. He turned back to Adelaide. "She died in childbirth."

Josiah thought Adelaide's face looked flushed. Was she angry? Upset? Of course, she was upset. How could he think otherwise?

She eyed him warily. "Where is the child?"

"I'm told she's at an orphanage in Bayview, Massachusetts."

"She."

He nodded.

"Does she have a name?"

Her question startled him. He hadn't even thought of that. "I suppose she does. I just don't know what it is."

"How old is she?"

"Three."

"What do you plan to do?"

He thought for a moment. "I have to get her." He looked at Adelaide for understanding. "She's my flesh and blood."

"You had no idea?"

He was puzzled by her question. "No, of course not. What? You think I would keep something like this from you?"

"I don't know what to think anymore, Josiah." Her voice was thick with defeat. "Besides, you don't owe me an explanation." She glanced at her hands and whispered, "After all, I'm just your cook." She looked up at him.

Her words hurt. He thought they had grown closer. But maybe that was all on his part. "Is that the way you want it?"

"Well, that was the agreement."

"Yes, I suppose it was," he answered, wishing with all his

heart he could change things.

"When will you get her?"

He stroked his chin. "I don't know. I'll have to check into it."

"I see."

He paused a moment. "Will you go with me?"

Adelaide swallowed hard. "I'll have to think on that, Josiah. I committed to being your cook, but a mother? Well, I just don't know."

He nodded. "We'll talk later."

છ

Now it was Adelaide's turn to walk. Though it wasn't proper to appear on the streets unescorted, Adelaide didn't care. She needed time to think.

Alone.

The beauty of the sights around her did little to lift her spirits. It's not that she minded mothering a child, especially Josiah's child, but she couldn't help feeling—what was it? She took a deep breath. "Might as well call it what it is, Adelaide Sanborn Buchanan. Jealousy." The thought shamed her, but she knew it was true.

She was jealous of Catherine. No matter how hard she tried to rationalize her feelings, she knew the root of the problem. Catherine owned a piece of Josiah's heart that Adelaide felt certain she could never reach. Perhaps Catherine owned all of his heart. Adelaide wondered if he'd ever offer his love to her.

Each time it seemed they were drawing closer, something would happen to make him pull away. The only thing she could imagine to hold him back was Catherine.

How can I compete with memories? What do I do when the "other woman" is no longer living? Josiah's love is buried with Catherine, and I have to accept it.

Stopping for a moment, Adelaide reached for a seashell that had found its way a distance from the shore. She turned it over in her palm, examining the tiny crevices.

She straightened and held the shell in her hand. She decided to keep it. Most likely, she would never come to the island again.

Choices. How much she had learned about choices. Why hadn't she sought God's heart before saying yes to Josiah? Would He have led her to marry him? Would He have whispered no to her heart? Her footsteps carried her to a large rock. She sat upon it. The ocean waves stirred with a slight wind. Sounds of the sea calmed her spirit.

How could she be so cold as to turn down mothering Josiah's daughter just because the little girl belonged to another woman? There was no doubt in Adelaide's mind she could and would love the child. What she feared was if the girl looked like Catherine. Would the resemblance be a constant reminder to Josiah of his love for his late wife? Could Adelaide bear to always live in the shadow of another?

Hot tears stung her eyes. She swiped at the tears with the back of her hand. Why couldn't she be strong? She knew Josiah cared about her, but he had never indicated he loved her. If only Adelaide knew that Josiah loved her, she could bear it all, but as it was, she felt like nothing more than a hired servant.

"Oh, Ma, I wish you were here. You'd know right what to do." Her thoughts wrestled with her heart.

"Adelaide!"

She turned on the rock to see Adam running her way. Dabbing once more at her face, she rose and walked toward him. A broad grin stretched across his face.

"Adam, what is it?"

He waved some envelopes. "We've got mail."

Energy pumped through her. She clasped her hands together.

"You got one from Esther, and I got one as well," he said with a hint of boasting.

"Is that a fact?" she asked with a smile, hiding the turmoil in her heart.

"Josiah asked that I bring this to you if I saw you. He's tending to some repairs on the ship."

She nodded. "Thank you so much, Adam."

He handed her the envelope. "Well, I know you're anxious to read the letter, so I'll leave you be and let you enjoy the news from home." He smiled again and left her.

Adelaide headed back to her rock and settled into a comfortable position. She looked at the envelope and wondered why her mother hadn't written. Most likely, they both had written and sent it in one envelope, she decided. Anxiously, she tore it open:

Dearest Adelaide,

I trust this letter finds you well. How we miss you! Our home is much too quiet since you've gone. Ma misses you something fierce. She tries to act brave, but you know how she is. It helps her to know you are happy with Josiah.

Guilt pinched Adelaide's heart. She read on.

I regret, dear sister, to tell you Ma is not well.

Adelaide's breath caught in her throat.

She has a bad cough. Doctor says it's consumption.

Adelaide wiped tears from her eyes once more.

I didn't want to tell you, but we fear she is getting worse, and, well, I didn't know if you could get home to see her. Perhaps it is impossible to do so, but I wanted to try to reach you so you would have the choice.

The rest of the letter was lost to Adelaide. She folded it and allowed the tears to freely flow. Too many choices already. Now she must make another. She had to get to Ma. But how? What would Josiah say? Could they make arrangements?

She lifted a piece of her skirt to her face and dried her eyes. "Enough feeling sorry for yourself." Adelaide looked at the sea once more and stood to her feet. She knew what she had to do.

sixteen

Though Adelaide's emotions got the better of her at times, once she made up her mind about something, the matter was settled. Sometimes to her detriment. She pushed the thoughts of Catherine, Josiah, and "their daughter" aside. For now, she had to concentrate on getting home to her ma.

She walked back to the cottage. Upon entering, she found Josiah waiting on the sofa, arms folded across his chest, his mouth drawn in a tight line.

"Where have you been?" His words held a father's discipline.

Anger worked its way up her spine. "I've been thinking." She looked him square in the face. "If you must know."

He stood. She could see his chest rise and fall with each breath. "Adelaide, you know it's not proper for a woman to walk the streets unescorted. Especially in an unknown land."

She gritted her teeth. "I care nothing about propriety today, Josiah. I needed time to think."

He took a few steps toward her.

She stepped back. "I'm going home." She said the words more sharply than she had intended.

He stopped. His eyes widened. His gaze never left her face. She felt a stab of regret. It's not that she wanted to hurt him. She just needed time to think things through. More importantly, she needed to get home to Ma.

"I see." His gaze dropped to the floor, as if searching for what to say next.

"Ma's sick."

He looked back to her. "The letter?"

"Yes."

He cautiously took a couple of steps toward her again; still she backed away. She didn't want his nearness to cloud her thinking. He stopped again, a look of sympathy on his face. The last thing she wanted was his pity. She could tell he hadn't expected the wall between them. Sorrow tugged at her heart.

"You wish to travel alone?"

She nodded.

"I won't let you go on just any ship." His words left no room for argument. "You are my wife—"

"Your cook," she corrected.

"And my wife." The tone of his voice told her not to argue, which, of course, made her want to all the more. But she resisted the urge.

"I'll go to the docks this afternoon and see if I can find an appropriate ship on which you can sail home."

She couldn't make herself look at him.

"Adelaide, I. . ." He reached his arm out to her.

"I need to get things packed," she said, turning away from him. As much as it pained her to do so, she couldn't deal with any more talk. Not now.

Stepping away, she wondered if there was anything more painful than a breaking heart.

❧

The next morning, Josiah walked the streets toward the wharf. Salty comments and raucous laughter seeped through the air from the town's saloon. Those sounds ultimately gave way to carpenters' tools, scrubbing, and fragmented conversations as men worked on the ships in dock. Strange-looking birds called from a clear blue sky. Josiah barely noticed. His thoughts grew darker with every step.

He hadn't expected Adelaide to be so unfeeling about the news of his child. She was softhearted and kind—or so he thought. Of course, he had been wrong before. But that was another woman, another time.

Was it so terrible for Adelaide to think of watching over his child? Did she despise him that much? A thought struck him. Maybe she didn't like children. Surely that would not be the case. He had seen her with the children at church, and she seemed delighted to spend time with them. No, that couldn't be it.

His boots shuffled against the dirt road, kicking up dust behind him. A cloud of despair seemed to follow him to the dock. He wasn't sure if he felt discouraged or angry. After all, why wouldn't she care for his child? If Adelaide could not love his child, he certainly could not love Adelaide! Trouble was, he already did love her. Would she take his love and cast it aside the way Catherine had?

He shook the thought from his head. Well, he would not let her go traipsing halfway across the globe in just any old ship, whether she liked it or not. She was his wife, and he aimed to see her safely home. He made the decision then and there to go with her as far as Bayview. Her headstrong ways would get her into trouble one day but not as long as he could help it.

Josiah made his way from ship to ship, asking where each one was bound, losing all hope of getting Adelaide home until he came upon the next to the last one. He found the *Wallace* was headed for Panama City. He talked to the captain and, through the course of the conversation, found they had a cabin that would house one guest, and Josiah could bunk out with the crew. Not ideal, but at least they could get as far as Panama City. They would have to book passage on the railroad in hopes to catch a clipper in the port of Colon on the Caribbean side. Josiah discussed the trip with the captain, and they agreed upon an appropriate price. Josiah also agreed to help with any whaling endeavors.

Relieved to have that matter taken care of, Josiah decided his next step would be to talk to his first mate about taking over the *Courage* in his absence. Though at first Josiah had refused to see it, Adam Bowman had proven himself a worthy seaman time and again. Josiah had no doubt the man could handle the ship. Granting Adam the captain's position would increase his pay substantially and possibly give him the savings he needed to go home and ask for Esther's hand in marriage. Josiah felt a twinge of envy. If only Adelaide cared about him the same way.

He stooped to pick up a pebble and threw it across the beach—something he did as a child when he was angry. Funny he would think of that now. Somehow, rubbing the smooth stone and throwing it made him feel better. He wasn't sure why. Maybe he liked having control over something. Even if it was only a pebble. He certainly didn't feel in control of anything else in his life. He'd made a mess of things, and he knew it.

The Lord would help him through, but Josiah knew his choices brought consequences. He would pray for guidance in dealing with them.

He turned his thoughts back toward Adam. If Adam agreed to the change, Josiah would send the necessary message to the owners of the ship and settle up the money later. Josiah would sell what oil he could in port and give Adam the instructions for his trip to the Sandwich Islands.

He breathed a sigh of relief to have their trip scheduled. Most likely, Adelaide would be upset once she learned he would be traveling with her. Even the fiercest of whales were easier to tackle than her stubborn ways.

Seemed like she could be a little more understanding about things. He replayed the events of the past several months in his mind. Her life had changed dramatically since he entered it. He couldn't deny that. But then again, he hadn't forced her to marry him. She did so of her own accord. She wanted to sail. He gave her that chance. Did that make him so bad?

How absurd to try and fool himself. He knew his selfishness had brought on the current dilemma. His mind had told him he needed a cook, and Adelaide seemed the perfect solution. He hadn't stopped to consider it was really his heart dictating the marriage idea.

What did it matter how or where the idea germinated? Josiah knew that he loved Adelaide and readily admitted her help as cook on the ship had proved invaluable.

Now with the problem of his waning strength, the idea of leaving the whaling profession seemed a very real possibility. He knew for sure he would lose Adelaide if he stripped her of the one thing she wanted most—to sail the seas. He had ruined her dreams and his own as well.

No point in rethinking it. Maybe wrong choices had brought him to this place, but with the Lord's help, Josiah could make right choices for their future. He didn't know how he could fix things with Adelaide or if they could have a future together; he knew only that he would do whatever it took to make a life with her.

With nothing settled, yet a lighter heart, he walked toward the cottage.

But not before throwing one more pebble.

a

Josiah spent the next day helping his crew make some minor repairs to the ship. They also gave the deck a good scrubbing to prepare for sailing.

Adam was more than willing to take charge of the *Courage*. He all but puffed up like a rooster when Josiah presented the idea. At least that matter was settled. With the post sent informing the owners of the change, Josiah could rest a bit easier.

By early evening, Josiah started back toward the cottage to discuss Adelaide's departure. She was already in bed when he had gotten home the night before. With no opportunity to advise her of his news, he needed to get the information to her so she could pack. Would she look forward to leaving for more reasons than just seeing her ma?

He couldn't think about it. Too many problems cluttered

his mind. The matter of his child surfaced. His daughter. Hard to imagine himself as a pa. With his own pa gone on a whaling ship for months at a time, Josiah had little example of what a pa should be. If he continued on the *Courage*, he would be the same kind of pa for his child. A pa who was never around. Was that what he wanted?

What was he thinking? He could hardly change his whole career for this child he didn't know. After all, what else would he do? Whaling had been his life up to now. Much as it frightened him to admit it, he couldn't deny his weakness since the fever. He feared his whaling days were changing, but did he possess skills for any other profession? He couldn't imagine what it would be if he did. His head hurt from thinking.

Before his thoughts could travel further, he arrived at the cottage. He pushed through the doors and found Adelaide sitting on the sofa. She looked up from her sewing.

"Do you have a moment to talk?"

She nodded and laid the cloth in a nearby basket, carefully winding the thread and tucking the needle into the material. Once finished, with her hands folded in her lap, she turned her full attention to him.

"Hear me out before you say anything."

Though her expression revealed her curiosity, she merely nodded.

"I have found a ship on which you can sail to get home."

He noticed the way her eyes lit up when he mentioned going home. Had she hated life on the sea after all? Or was it life with him she despised?

"The thing is. . ." He measured his words carefully. "I'm going with you."

"You can't go with me," she protested.

He held up the palm of his hand. "Before you say anything else, let me tell you I'm going only as far as Bayview to pick up my daughter." Saying those words sounded foreign to his ears, as if someone else were saying them.

"I see."

What flashed across her face: disappointment, sorrow? Why? Because he was going along? "Adam will take over the *Courage.*"

A slight smile played on her lips. "That's nice for Adam."

"I thought it might help out his plans with Esther."

Adelaide almost seemed to soften. Josiah wanted to run to her, pull her into his arms, and tell her he loved her. How could he bear her going on to Yorksville? He couldn't lose her. He just couldn't. Neither could he ignore his own flesh and blood. Would Adelaide make him choose?

"Will you be able to meet up with the *Courage* later?"

Josiah nodded. "I expect so. I'll worry about that after I see what's ahead for me." Their gazes held as if they both considered their futures might lead them in different directions.

"How far will it take us?"

"Panama City. From there we will board the railroad and take it to the port of Colon on the Caribbean side. At that point, we'll catch a clipper and head for home."

She nodded.

"One other thing. I thought you might like to know the captain's wife, Elizabeth, and their five-year-old daughter, Emma, are traveling with him." He knew the idea of female companionship would please her.

"Wonderful!" She clasped her hands together, then as though she'd thought better of it, put on a serious face.

He stared at her. When she glanced up at him, he didn't turn away. "Once you leave for Yorksville, I will miss you, Adelaide." He didn't like revealing his heart to her, but the words were spoken before he could stop them. Josiah wanted to ask her not to go, fearing he would never see her again.

She looked as though she were about to say something, then thought better of it. "What will Adam do for a cook?"

He shrugged. "One of the crewmen. That's how other ships do it, anyway. Just whoever happens along, they pick to be cook. That's why I wanted you. I never liked running a ship that way. Meals are important to the crew. They work better when they eat well."

She nodded. "When do we sail?"

"Tomorrow. It will still be a long trip home but quicker than the *Courage* could have taken you." Josiah saw the worry on her face. "You'll make it in time, Adelaide. I'll be praying."

"Thank you."

He saw a tear trickle down her cheek. He wanted to go to her but feared her reaction. "I guess I'll leave you to your sewing. Just wanted you to know the arrangements had been made."

Adelaide bent over to pick up the material once again. "I appreciate your efforts, Josiah."

He tipped his head toward her, then walked out of the cottage.

❧

With skilled fingers, Adelaide poked the needle through the material, her thoughts clearly not on sewing. She stabbed her finger. "Oh, why do I always do that?" Blood squeezed through the tip of her index finger. Adelaide grabbed a scrap of cloth and held it on the small wound.

So Josiah would be sailing with her. Though she wanted time alone to think, she had to admit she welcomed his presence on a strange ship. Dangers lurked on such vessels, especially for women. The thought of his accompanying her calmed her somewhat.

Life was full of changes. Certainly, she had seen many changes in the past four months. Marriage. Moving from land to sea. Now Ma was sick. The very idea of all of it overwhelmed her.

Adelaide checked her finger. The bleeding had stopped. She folded the soiled cloth and tucked it in the basket to dispose of later. How could she sit still? Sunshine burst through the windows, and she decided she'd sit out in the yard, allowing the sea to calm her frazzled nerves. With all she had to do, though, she thought it best to pack first, then go outside.

She didn't have much to gather. She had learned quickly the value of packing light. Living on a ship, space was at a premium.

With the packing completed, Adelaide walked outside with a cup of tea. She settled into her chair and tried to shut out the thoughts racing across her mind.

In spite of her anxiety, she could hardly wait to see Ma and Esther again. A shadow of fear lurked in her thoughts. "God, please let me make it in time."

"Good day, Mrs. Buchanan."

Adelaide turned to see Adam standing there. "Hello, Adam. Please join me." She pointed to a nearby chair.

"Thank you." He grabbed the chair and pulled it over near her.

"I understand you've accepted a new position?"

A broad grin lined his face. "Yes, indeed. I sure appreciate Captain giving me this opportunity."

"He has utmost confidence in you," she assured him.

Adam cracked his knuckles. "I hope I don't let him down."

"You won't. You're good at what you do, and the men respect you. That's half the battle."

He nodded. "Sorry to hear about your ma."

"Thank you. I'm praying she'll get better and that I make it home to see her before. . ." She couldn't finish.

"I'll be praying, too." A catamaran drifted by in the distance. "I hope to see Esther when I get back."

Adelaide eyed him carefully. Something in his manner told her he had more to say.

He let the comment hover in the air. "Do you think she'll wait on me?" It took a full minute before he looked at her, as if her expression might tell him what he didn't want to know.

Adelaide smiled. "Well, I can't speak for Esther, but I know she cares a lot for you, Adam."

He let out a sigh as if he had been holding his breath.

Adelaide laughed. "You worry too much."

He took off his hat and smoothed his hair. "I guess I do." The sea glistened before them; large birds called from thick leafy trees. "When you go home, maybe you could let her know how I feel?"

"I would be happy to let her know."

He slapped his hands on his trousers. "I appreciate it, Addie—I mean, Mrs. Buchanan." He stood.

Adelaide had to hide a chuckle. Obviously, Adam had come merely to make sure she delivered his message. Esther was quite fortunate to have someone love her that way. How Adelaide longed for the same feelings from Josiah.

"You have a safe journey home. I hope to see you in about six to eight months."

"Be safe, Adam. We'll see you then." Watching him leave, Adelaide wondered what her life would be like when next she saw Adam Bowman.

seventeen

Six weeks into her trip, Adelaide grew more impatient to get to her ma with every passing day. They'd caught a couple of whales on the way, keeping Josiah busy with the crew. Since Adelaide roomed in the guest cabin and Josiah bunked with the sailors, she spent most of her time with Elizabeth McCord, the captain's wife.

Adelaide stretched on the chair in her cabin. She liked not having to prepare all the meals, though she did miss the *Courage*'s crew. She prayed for them daily. She also missed Josiah. Yet she knew she couldn't go back to him as a cook and pretend wife. As much as she wanted to be near him, she couldn't go on pretending. She loved him, plain and simple. It hurt too much to pretend otherwise. If Josiah declared his love to her, Adelaide would embrace his child with open arms. But to offer her life to him and his child purely as a hired hand, she couldn't bear it.

Adelaide refocused on the page of the book she held in her hands. How many times she had read the same words, she didn't know. She decided to give up and snapped the book shut. A knock sounded at the door. Smoothing her hair, Adelaide walked over to answer it. Elizabeth stood in the doorway. Five-year-old Emma stood bedside her mother, clutching the tattered doll known as Mrs. Plum firmly in her arms.

"Well, good morning," Adelaide said with a smile. "Do come in."

"I hope we're not disturbing you," Elizabeth said, ushering Emma in ahead of her.

"Not at all. You know I look forward to our visits." Once

they stepped through the entrance, Adelaide closed the door behind them.

Elizabeth sat in the extra chair her husband had placed in the cramped quarters so his wife and Adelaide could visit. With Adelaide's permission, Emma sat on the edge of the bed with Mrs. Plum. Elizabeth untied her bonnet and pulled it off. She plucked a handkerchief from her dress pocket and wiped the perspiration from her face. "It is so hot on deck today. Not much better down here."

"But at least we can cool off with water from the basin," Adelaide said, pointing toward the pitcher and bowl on the dresser.

Elizabeth nodded.

Pulling open her trunk, Adelaide lifted out a couple of children's books she had purchased on the island. Knowing the McCords had a child, she decided it would be nice to have the books on hand. Adelaide extended them to Emma and was delighted when the child's face perked up at the sight of them. Emma carefully placed Mrs. Plum beside her on the bed and reached for the books. "Thank you, Mrs. Buchanan." Hearing Josiah's name linked to hers made it hard to swallow.

"You're welcome." Adelaide sat down in her chair across from Elizabeth.

"You all right?"

Nothing got past Elizabeth. In their six weeks of traveling together, there wasn't much they hadn't learned about one another. Their friendship had blossomed from the start.

"I'm fine."

"You know you can't fool me, Adelaide Buchanan."

Adelaide tossed her a weak smile.

"You don't see him much on this ship, do you?" Elizabeth said the words in such a comforting way, Adelaide wanted to cry.

Instead she shook her head and swallowed hard to push away the knot in her throat.

Elizabeth reached out and patted Adelaide's arm. "Why don't you tell him how you feel?"

Adelaide sat staring at her lap. "I can't."

"Tell me why."

Elizabeth had a no-nonsense approach to life. She didn't allow her emotions to get all jumbled up with her good sense. Adelaide wished she could do that, but she couldn't separate the two. "You know why."

"I know that *you* say Josiah's still in love with his first wife, Catherine, but I'm not convinced."

Adelaide wiped her nose on a handkerchief and looked up with surprise.

Elizabeth shrugged. "Well, I'm not. I watched him as you came aboard ship, each going to your own rooms, the sadness in his eyes. I would never have guessed—"

"It's all part of the pretense."

"Adelaide, what I saw wasn't pretense. I could see love in his eyes. And fear."

Adelaide tried to understand what Elizabeth meant by that.

"At the time, I thought he feared being away from you, letting you out of his sight. Now I think he fears losing you forever."

"If only that were true."

"It is true. Why can't you believe me?" Elizabeth pulled a wrapped biscuit from her second dress pocket. "Want some, Emma?"

The child nodded her head, causing her golden curls to dance upon her shoulders. Elizabeth walked over, handed Emma part of the biscuit, then sat back down. "Adelaide?" she asked, extending a portion of the biscuit.

"No, thank you."

Elizabeth shrugged and bit into her half. "You know," she said between bites, "I live with a ship full of men, and I think I know a little about the male species."

Adelaide chuckled in spite of herself. Though Elizabeth was ten years older, Adelaide loved the woman dearly. The men respected her, and Elizabeth treated them as if each one were her brother.

"I've heard more love stories than I can count, and I can tell you if a man's in love a mile away." She waved her biscuit for emphasis, dropping a crumb or two in the process. "It's written all over his face." She took another bite and chewed heartily. "That's the look I saw on Josiah."

How the words warmed Adelaide's heart. She wanted desperately to cling to them. They offered her the hope for which her heart longed.

"Write him a letter."

Adelaide bit her lip. "I don't know if I can." She paused a moment. "Besides, he's said nothing of coming to get me. We've made no arrangements to meet." Her voice began to rise in pitch with each word. "Once he gets to Bayview, I have no idea if I'll ever see him again."

Elizabeth grinned. "You'll see him."

Adelaide blew out a sigh. "I hope you're right, Elizabeth. Still, I will go only if he wants me for a true wife. I can no longer bear to serve as merely a helper."

Elizabeth laughed and shook her head. "Anyone ever tell you you're stubborn?"

"Too many to count."

"Well, you can add my name to the list."

Adelaide smiled and sent up a prayer of thanks for her friend, who managed to lighten many a dreary day.

❧

The days were long, and the nights were longer. Josiah wondered how much more loneliness he could endure. After Catherine had left him, his days had seemed hollow and empty. Yet those days paled in comparison to what he experienced now. Without an appetite, he forced himself to eat enough to get by. His stomach churned, and his heart hurt in a way he couldn't put into words. He stood at the railing and stared out to sea.

He made only enough contact with Adelaide to keep the rest of the crew away from her. They barely talked, neither knowing what to say. He didn't like the idea of a future without Adelaide. He wanted to let her know, but pride stopped him. She didn't love him. The fact that she couldn't bear the thought of raising his child proved that.

Nothing made sense to him anymore. He'd go pick up his daughter in Bayview and decide what to do from there. But first he had to think about obtaining passage on the railroad once they arrived in Panama City. Another two weeks should most likely get them there. A little more time left to decide what he would do. How could he win her heart?

"Hello, Josiah."

He turned around and saw Adelaide standing a few feet from him. His heart beat like a blackfish thumping in his chest. "How are you, Adelaide?"

"I'm fine. And you?"

"Good."

She walked up beside him and leaned on the rail with him. "It never ceases to take my breath away."

He stared at her. "Me, neither."

She looked at him. He kept his gaze fixed on her, without a single blink. Could she tell he wanted to hold her next to him and never let her go, to feel the warmth of her lips pressed hard against his? She turned away. He sighed and turned back to the sea. "Should get there in a couple of weeks."

Adelaide said nothing. Josiah figured she just wanted to get the whole thing over. What a mess he had made of everything. She probably couldn't get home fast enough, for more reasons than just seeing her ma. "I'll get you there quick as I can, Adelaide."

She placed a hand on his arm. "I know, Josiah, and I'm so very thankful for your help."

The brush of her hand sent currents through him like the touch of an electric eel. Torture. That's what she was putting him through, pure torture. Dare he ask her what was to become of them in the days ahead? The mere thought of approaching the subject turned his gut to the consistency of melting whale blubber. He couldn't ask her. Not yet. He couldn't bear to hear what was sure to come. But soon. He'd ask her soon, for he had to know.

๖

Adelaide would miss Elizabeth and Emma once they docked. She could hardly believe they'd be in Panama City in less than twenty-four hours. She prayed she would reach her ma in time.

"Adelaide." With Emma tagging along behind, Elizabeth walked up to Adelaide on the deck. Mrs. Plum dangled at Emma's side. A chicken clucked across the deck, catching the girl's attention.

"Can I play with Henny, Mama?"

"Stay where I can see you, Emma. And don't get in the way of the workers."

"Yes, Mama." Mrs. Plum's cloth body bobbed against Emma's legs as she skipped off toward the strutting chicken.

Elizabeth turned to Adelaide. "Are you all packed?"

"Yes. Wasn't much to do, really."

Elizabeth nodded, her mood pensive.

"You all right?"

Elizabeth smiled weakly. She waited. Sounds of the sea, the hum of men shuffling about the ship, and Emma muttering to Henny filled the air. "I'll miss you terribly," Elizabeth finally managed. Tears filled her eyes.

"Oh!" Adelaide reached over and wrapped her friend in an immense embrace. "I will miss you, too, Elizabeth. You have been such a wonderful friend!" They hugged a moment more, then pulled apart.

"Aren't we behaving like silly women?" Elizabeth asked, dabbing at her eyes with a handkerchief.

Adelaide laughed, wiping at her own wet cheeks.

"Whoa there, you two. I'll have none of that on my ship." Peter McCord took broad steps toward them. Josiah walked along beside him. Adelaide's pulse quickened.

Shaggy gray eyebrows lifted as Peter McCord smiled tenderly toward his wife. There was something in that smile that warmed Adelaide's heart. Peter's love for Elizabeth was written all over his face. Was that what Elizabeth was talking about? Is that what she had seen in Josiah?

Adelaide dared a glance at Josiah. His eyes were studying her. She felt herself blush.

Elizabeth must have recognized the awkward moment, for she was the first to speak. "I was just telling Adelaide how much I would miss her."

Adelaide looked up to see Josiah still staring at her. This time he nodded his head in agreement. Would he miss her, too? Oh, she had to quit torturing herself.

Straightening the cuff of her sleeve, she looked at Elizabeth, though she could still feel Josiah's gaze upon her. She felt restless beneath his stare.

"Are you packed?" Josiah's voice held such tenderness, Adelaide couldn't help but look at him.

She nodded. "Are you?"

His gaze fixed on her, he nodded. For a moment, it felt as though they were the only two people on the ship. She could almost imagine Josiah reaching out to her, pulling her to him, ever so gently lifting off her bonnet and kissing her right temple, his soft lips eventually making their way to her mouth, claiming it tenderly yet firmly with his own.

A burning seared through her. She actually touched her cheeks, feeling the warmth in them. Whatever was she thinking? She mentally shook herself. Josiah smiled at her as if he knew exactly where her thoughts had taken her.

Someone had said something, but Adelaide missed it. When her eyes refocused, the entire little group was looking at her. "I'm sorry?" she asked, looking at Elizabeth.

Elizabeth threw her a knowing grin. "Actually, Peter was just saying he thought the weather would hold out for your arrival in Panama City." Elizabeth looked as though she were hiding a giggle behind her hand.

Adelaide couldn't leave the group fast enough. "Well, I really need to finish a few things in my room. If you'll excuse me." Before anyone could respond, she turned and walked across the deck, feeling sure they were still watching her.

❧

In no time at all, Adelaide and Josiah stood in the hot afternoon sun, saying their good-byes to the McCords. Among tears and promises to keep in touch, the women finally separated. The McCords boarded the ship, and Josiah led Adelaide to a carriage that would take them to the train station.

Adelaide settled into her seat and tried not to think about the friend she had left behind. She took a deep breath. The stifling air made it hard to breathe. Grabbing her container of water, she took a drink. The carriage ride proved bumpy and a bit unpleasant as they jostled their way to the station. Adelaide didn't feel much like talking, and Josiah seemed to sense it. They said very little during the ride.

Once they arrived, Adelaide watched the scores of people milling around the station. The place buzzed with activity. Josiah purchased their tickets, and he and Adelaide stepped across the wooden platform to board the train.

"You hungry?"

"I think I'm too tired to eat."

"We'll need to get something soon, though. Why don't you try and get some rest? We can eat later."

Adelaide lifted a tired smile. She appreciated how he took care of her, especially now, yet she couldn't help feeling he was desperate to get her to watch his child. Who else could he turn to for fulfilling that responsibility while he ran a ship? She almost bolted straight up in her chair. Did he expect her to stay behind on land and watch his daughter while he traveled the seas? The very idea made her blood boil.

No doubt about it, he was being nice to her so she would watch his child while he continued to go whaling. She didn't like this at all.

When she looked over at Josiah, his gaze caught hers, and he smiled. Oh, she could see beneath his innocent exterior. She forced herself to turn away and watch the scenery that flew by the window.

She could hardly wait to get home.

eighteen

The railroad trip passed in a blur. Though she'd never ridden a train before, Adelaide had enjoyed the sights and the experience.

She could hardly believe she and Josiah were now sailing the Caribbean. They had boarded a clipper in Colon, South America. Their next destination was the waters of the Atlantic and home.

The speed of the clipper amazed Adelaide. The *Courage* could not compare to it. She wondered what man would come up with in the future for travel. Certainly improvements were being made daily.

Though thrown together in a cabin, Josiah and Adelaide spent little time there. She avoided him whenever possible. She didn't need him around to confuse her further. He seemed to know she needed her space and gave it to her. How could she think when he stood close to her or when she looked into the blue eyes that made her knees buckle? Sometimes, the very way he spoke her name took her breath away.

No, she needed space. Lots of it. The sooner he got off at Bayview, the better. Still, the very idea punctured her heart with pain.

❧

The days melted one on top of the other. Josiah could hardly believe they were pulling into the Bayview port. He watched as the ship clumsily made its way to the deep harbor. After all these weeks, he was no closer to changing Adelaide's mind than from the start. Their interaction had been minimal since they left the island. Formal and distant, at best.

Adelaide walked up behind him. "You've got all your things?"

He turned to her and nodded. Neither had said anything about where they would go from here. Every time he had tried to approach the subject, she cut him off, telling him she needed time to think. He wondered if he'd ever see her again.

"I hope you find your daughter," Adelaide said almost in a whisper.

The wind caused a wisp of a curl to dance upon her cheek. Before he caught himself, Josiah reached over and tucked it gently behind her bonnet. Their eyes locked. "Look, Adelaide, I know our situation isn't the best—"

"Please, Josiah. Don't." Tears filled her eyes. "We both need some time."

He asked the question to which he feared the answer. "When will I hear from you?" A sadness such as he had never known gripped his heart like a heavy clamp. So many words left unsaid. They clogged his throat, trying to break free, but he knew it wouldn't make a difference. Not now. He swallowed them.

Adelaide stared at him. "I don't know." A tear rolled down her cheek.

What held her back? Had he been wrong about her love for him, or was she being stubborn? The idea that she would allow her stubbornness to keep them apart made him angry, making it easier to let her go. If her love didn't go any deeper than that, she would never be happy raising his child or living out her days with him. Somehow knowing that gave him the strength to release her.

"I hope you find what you want, Adelaide." Without another word, Josiah picked up his trunk, turned, and walked away.

❧

Scenes of Josiah's departure haunted Adelaide's mind time after time. Today, though, she refused to think about it. For this day would bring her joy or great sorrow. She would either see her ma or learn of her death.

Standing on the deck, Adelaide anxiously awaited the opportunity to step onto Yorksville's shores. Through the light fog, she could just make out Markle's General Store in the distance. July brought summer into full bloom, and despite her aching heart, Adelaide could hardly wait for the ship to dock.

It seemed an eternity, but she finally stepped onto the land, and her heart swelled with thankfulness and a prayer that her ma was still alive. She wanted to pop in and see the Markles but felt she had to get straight home. She didn't want to hear bad news, if there was any, from anyone but family. A kind couple offered her a ride in their carriage, and she was home in no time. At the edge of their property, Adelaide gathered her things, then stood and faced the house. She took a deep breath and made her way toward the front door. Before she could get there, a scream sounded behind her.

"Addie!" Esther came running from the henhouse as fast as her long skirts would allow.

Adelaide dropped her trunk and ran to her sister. They embraced and cried tears of joy. When the excitement died down, Adelaide pulled away, looked her sister square in the face, and asked the question that had plagued her for months. She pulled in a ragged breath. "Ma?"

Esther turned toward the house. Adelaide's eyes followed until they stopped at a form standing just outside the front door. Adelaide's blurry eyes focused. "Ma!" she cried, running to her. When she reached Ma, Adelaide pulled her into a firm hug, never wanting to let go. She was alarmed at the frailty of her ma's body beneath her arms, but Adelaide would not let that steal her joy for now. She'd made it home to her family, and that's what mattered.

She looked at her ma's tired eyes and quickly escorted her toward the door. "We have much to catch up on, Ma. Let's get you inside for a long visit."

Ma wiped the tears from her face and nodded. A smiling Esther walked beside them.

Once inside the house, Esther set to making tea while

Adelaide and Ma settled into chairs in the living room. Ma told of her near-death experience and how God had brought her through. Though she struggled with weakness, she felt her strength returning day by day, and they all rejoiced in her healing.

Adelaide shared of her life on the seas. Esther sat across from them, starry-eyed as always, while Ma listened with interest. Adelaide felt uncomfortable under Ma's gaze. Ma knew her all too well, and Adelaide had no doubts Ma could read much into what wasn't being said.

To quickly change the subject, Adelaide told Esther of Adam's feelings for her. "Oh, I almost forgot!" Adelaide shot up from her chair and ran over to her trunk. She searched through her things and pulled out a dainty package. Quickly, she closed the lid of the trunk and made her way to Esther. "He asked me to give this to you."

With wide eyes, Esther looked at Adelaide, then the package, then at Adelaide once again.

Adelaide shoved it toward her. "Well, are you going to take it, or do I have to stand here all day?"

Esther smiled and reached for it, quickly opening the package. Inside, she found a dainty gold necklace with a small turquoise stone dangling from it. Esther gasped and, with shaking fingers, pulled the necklace from its case. Adelaide helped her put it on.

"Well, that pretty much settles the matter," Ma said in her practical way. "She's had plenty of men calling, but Esther's been waiting for Adam." Ma cradled a cup of tea in her hands and shook her head.

"Well, I'd say he has plans for the two of you if you'll have him," Adelaide assured her.

"I suppose I'm losing another daughter to the sea," Ma said but quickly gave her blessing with a smile.

"There's never been anyone else for me from the day I first set eyes on him."

Another jab of pain struck Adelaide's heart. Oh, to have that kind of love for another and to be loved in return.

"And what of Josiah, Adelaide?" Though she knew Ma would ask the question sooner or later, Adelaide had hoped they could discuss it later.

"It's much too long a story, Ma. Can we talk about it later, after I've had some rest?" Adelaide didn't miss the eye contact between Ma and Esther.

"Certainly, dear. Why don't you go take a nap, and we'll have dinner prepared by the time you wake up."

"Oh, I couldn't have you do that—"

"You can and you will. Ma has spoken," Esther said with a laugh. She lifted one end of Adelaide's trunk and pulled it toward the bedroom.

Adelaide shrugged toward her ma and followed Esther.

&

Though she couldn't imagine how long she'd been in bed, Adelaide had to admit the nap felt good. She hadn't realized how exhausted she was from the trip. The wooden slats beneath her creaked when she stretched her body and let out a yawn. Reluctantly, she pulled herself from the comfortable bed and straightened herself. A quick glance in the looking glass told her more than she wanted to know. With a tuck here and there in her hairpins, she made herself presentable and went into the kitchen to help with dinner preparations.

"We're almost ready to eat," Ma told her. Adelaide felt ashamed of herself for sleeping while they did all the work. Ma must have read her mind.

"Now, don't you give it a thought, Adelaide. You had a long trip, and we're thrilled to have you home. I'll put you to work soon enough." Ma smiled.

They had a pleasant dinner and a nice visit. Adelaide shared more stories of her adventures, even telling them about Ebenezer Fallon. Ma shook her head and clicked her tongue, adding something about the ways of men.

Esther headed to a friend's house where several of the church ladies were gathering to work on a quilt, leaving Adelaide and Ma behind to do some serious talking.

They finally settled into chairs out in the front yard. The hot air did little to comfort them, but they hoped a slight breeze might stir among the trees.

Not being one to mince words, Ma came right out with it. "You want to tell me what's going on with you and Josiah?" Ma wiped the perspiration from her neck with a handkerchief.

Adelaide sighed before telling the story of her life for the past eight months. Of course, she left out the part of their deceit. She didn't want Ma to know her true reason for marrying Josiah. When she finished, Ma looked at her and said nothing. She could see more than Adelaide intended. Feeling a smidgen uncomfortable, Adelaide looked away and pretended to be interested in a bird that flew by. Ma had a way of knowing when her daughters didn't tell the entire truth, and Adelaide just didn't feel like explaining at present.

"When do you plan to return to him?"

Sometimes Adelaide wished Ma weren't so direct. Most likely, she wouldn't appreciate the answer, anyway. "I don't know."

Ma swatted at a bug that flew close to her face. Adelaide wondered if Ma took her present frustration out on the insect. "What's holding you back, Adelaide?"

"It's complicated, Ma."

She raised her eyebrows. "Too complicated for me to understand, is that what you mean?"

No response.

"Does he hurt you?"

Adelaide's head shot up. "Of course not! He's good to me. Well, Josiah's about the best—" She stopped midsentence when she realized Ma had baited her with the question, and Adelaide had fallen for it, rising to Josiah's defense in a heartbeat.

Ma smiled.

Mad at herself for falling prey to Ma's strategy, Adelaide kicked a stone from the ground under her feet. "I'm not ready for a child, Ma."

Ma nodded her head and looked in the distance. "Oh, I see. I didn't realize your wedding vows contained conditions. I must have missed that." She wiped her face again.

Adelaide blew out a frustrated sigh.

Ma turned to Adelaide once more. "Look, Adelaide, I can't tell you what to do. You're a grown woman with a life of your own. You need to search your heart and pray. Pray more than you've ever prayed in your life, because your future is at stake here. How you handle this situation will not only affect your life, but Josiah's and his daughter's as well. But hear me on this, Adelaide. You must return to him sometime. He is your husband."

Without looking up, Adelaide nodded.

"Enough of that," Ma said, brushing her hands together as if wiping the conversation from them. "Let's go pick out a chicken for tomorrow's dinner."

Killing and preparing a chicken for dinner had always been one of Adelaide's least favorite jobs, though after being on the whaling ship, she knew she had developed a stomach of cast iron. Very little made her squeamish these days.

When they entered the barn, chickens clucked and scattered about. From a bowl, Ma threw some feed on the ground, and the chickens greedily pecked their way through the tiny bits of food. Once the bowl was empty, Ma put it on a shelf, brushed her hands on the front of her dress, and pointed toward a fat chicken to her right. "I'm thinking tomorrow night's Mabel's night."

Adelaide groaned. "Ma, how many times do I have to tell you not to name them? I can't eat them if they have names."

Ma laughed until she saw the serious expression on Adelaide's face. "I'm sorry, honey. It's the way of life out here. You know that."

"I know. I just. . .well. . .don't like it."

"Adelaide, they were born to die. They serve their purpose to help us sustain life. That's the life to which they were called."

Adelaide didn't want to think. Seemed like every conversation weighed her down. She loved Ma, but she wanted to go off by herself.

"Why don't you hitch up the team and go into town for some sugar and flour? We're just about out. Besides, the Markles can hardly wait to see you."

The thought made her feel better. A journey to town might be just the thing she needed right now. She definitely wanted to visit with the Markles, anyway.

Adelaide hitched the horses to the buckboard and arrived in town fairly quickly. She stepped through the doors of Markle's General Store. The bell jangled overhead, but Adelaide's footsteps carried her into an empty room. Her boots seemed to echo upon the wooden floor. Adelaide glanced through the bolts of material and other goods on the shelves. She couldn't help noticing that things were not quite as neat and tidy as before. The Markles must keep too busy.

Upon hearing a stirring behind the counter, Adelaide turned around to see Mrs. Markle jotting something in the logbook.

"Good day, Mrs. Markle."

Mrs. Markle continued writing without lifting her head. "Oh, sorry, I didn't see anyone in here."

Feeling a bit giddy with the surprise, Adelaide quietly edged her way through the room while the storekeeper finished writing.

With the last stroke of the pen, Ida Markle laid it down and looked up. She gasped, jumped from her chair, and, with outstretched arms, made her way to Adelaide. "Oh, dear, dear Adelaide!" She pulled her into a tight hug, almost cutting off Adelaide's air supply. "How we've missed you!"

Adelaide struggled to catch her breath. "I've missed you, too," she finally managed in between coughs.

"Caleb, you've got to come out here and see who's meandering around our store."

Caleb poked his head around the corner. "Why, Adelaide Sanborn!" he crowed with a huge grin.

Ida Markle laughed. "It's Buchanan now, Caleb, did you forget?"

"Oh, I did, at that."

"How could you forget our girl running off and getting herself hitched like that?" The old woman looked around. "Where's the grand sea captain?"

An aching pain rolled through Adelaide. "He couldn't come. I came back to check on Ma."

"Oh, of course," Mrs. Markle said with a wave of her hand. She looked at Caleb. "Can we tell her?"

He nodded.

"It's an act of God that you are here, child. We've been talking about this place. We're not able to keep it up anymore. Now, we know you love the sea, and most likely, that's where you'll stay, but you walking in like a miracle—well, we just have to tell you. If you and Josiah should decide to settle on land, we'd like you to take over running the store. Caleb and me, well, we'd just live upstairs like we do now, but you could live in the downstairs apartment and the majority of ownership in the store would belong to you. We'd maintain only enough ownership to get us by. We'd always planned to give the store to you, anyway. You've been like a daughter to us."

Adelaide stared at them, speechless.

"Now, we don't want you feeling obligated. Like we said, we know you love the sea, so it probably won't work out for you. But seeing you walk in today and us just making the decision only yesterday to have someone take over, well, seemed like an answer to prayer."

They looked at her through eager eyes. Adelaide had no

idea what to say. "I—I don't know." Her mind raced in all directions. If she didn't go with Josiah, at least she'd have an income, and a mighty fine business at that. She loved working at the store facing the sea. But she knew that life would be without Josiah. The sea owned him.

"I'll have to give it much thought and talk it over with Josiah. I'll let you know. That's the best I can do."

They both smiled. "That's all we ask, dear, that you at least consider it and pray about it."

They chatted a little longer. Other townsfolk made their way into the store and visited with Adelaide. As she finally made her way home, she mulled over their generous offer. In many ways, it seemed the perfect solution. If she knew Josiah loved her, Adelaide could stay on land and raise his child there. Too bad Josiah couldn't give up whaling; the general store would provide a wonderful income and family life for them.

But, of course, that was silly. Everyone knew Josiah would sail the seas as long as he lived.

nineteen

Adelaide could hardly believe a week had passed since her arrival at Yorksville. It felt good to be home and see familiar faces. The townsfolk didn't seem to think it unusual she had come back without Josiah. After all, her ma was sick, and Josiah had a ship to run.

After finishing the dinner dishes, Adelaide took a walk around the property. All week, turmoil had churned bitterly in her stomach. Stopping in front of the henhouse, Adelaide thought about her mother's comment, *"They were born to die."* The phrase kept rolling over in her mind time and again.

She paced. Wasn't that true of herself as well? She was born to die to self. As a Christian, her life belonged to Jesus Christ. As she learned from the Lord and grew stronger in her Christian journey, His desires became her own.

So what of her current situation with Josiah? She walked amid clucking and strutting hens. They quickly pattered away as Adelaide moved closer.

"They live to die." No matter how she turned that phrase over in her mind, the truth of it burned in her soul. Josiah was a good man. He treated her well and had accepted Christ as his Savior. Whether he still loved Catherine or not shouldn't matter. Adelaide had agreed to be his wife knowing full well he had been married before.

Adelaide threw some chicken feed on the ground and watched the chickens cluster toward it. She didn't know how long she stayed there, praying over the matter, thinking, and finally deciding.

With the issue settled in her heart, Adelaide knew what she had to do. She turned and walked out of the henhouse with renewed determination and excitement. Tonight she would talk with Ma and Esther, and tomorrow she would make arrangements to go to Bayview in search of Josiah and his child. She only hoped she could make it before it was too late.

ↀ

By the time Josiah made it to the orphanage, he had little strength left. He knew he should have gotten a room first, but he couldn't wait a moment longer to see his child. Once inside, he sat on the nearest chair and rested a moment.

"May I help you?" A thin woman with a beak of a nose, small eyes, and a permanent wrinkle between her brows said the words with impatience.

Josiah thought she looked like a bird. Feeling as though he were back in school, he stood and pulled off his cap. "I'm here to pick up my daughter." He took the envelope from his pocket and handed it to her.

She glared at him, then pulled out the letter, reading over it briefly. Stuffing it back into the envelope, she looked back at him and eyed him suspiciously. "And just how do I know you're Josiah Buchanan?" Her lips were pulled into a severe line.

Though Josiah understood the reason for her question and appreciated her caution, Bird Woman was getting on his nerves. "I've got the letter, don't I?"

She harrumphed, clearly offended by his comment. The woman lifted her chin, turned, and walked away. Josiah decided he should follow. They entered a small room with a desk and two chairs. Without a window, the room appeared stark and depressing. Over the next hour, Bird Woman grilled him with questions and handed him endless papers to fill out. Finally seeming convinced of his identity, she stood and announced, "I'll take you to her."

"Before we go, I need to let you know that I'll have to make arrangements for a room at a boardinghouse, and I have some other matters to tend to, so I will return tomorrow evening for her. I trust she will be ready?"

The woman reluctantly nodded.

"Um, what's her name?"

She turned a condemning look at him, as though he should be ashamed for not knowing. How could he have known? He hadn't even known he had a child.

"Grace."

The name surprised him. He hadn't thought Catherine capable of choosing such a name. Josiah and the woman made their way to a room full of children preparing to eat dinner. Bird Woman went to the front of the room.

She clapped her hands together in the most annoying way, and the room grew quiet. "I wish to see Grace Buchanan, please."

Josiah's heart pounded hard against his chest. He searched the room for his daughter. Finally, the tiniest of forms with blond braided hair that fell to her waist walked away from the others and made her way toward Bird Woman. Josiah felt his legs go soft. As Grace walked toward him, he couldn't believe what he saw. A shrunken imitation of himself, though her features were softened by femininity. Not a shred of Catherine in her. For some reason, relief washed over him.

With her head lowered, Grace lifted cautious eyes to him as if peering over spectacles. She chewed on her thumbnail while standing a bit behind Bird Woman's skirt. The woman raised her chin and pulled Grace away from her. "Grace, this is your father, Captain Josiah Buchanan."

The little girl said nothing. Josiah decided he would stay in Bayview for a short while, in an environment with which she was familiar, to give them time to get acquainted. He knew it would take some doing, but somehow he would win Grace's heart, and he would treasure raising her.

With or without Adelaide.

❧

Though tired and spent from her trip to Bayview, Adelaide still had time to make it to the orphanage before nightfall.

When she arrived, a lady there told her Josiah had picked up his child, and most likely they had set sail by now.

Exhaustion made her want to cry. But instead, Adelaide merely thanked the woman and made her way out the door. What would she do? Ma had given her some money so she could at least spend the night if she could find a room. Tomorrow she would have to make her way back to Yorksville. Alone.

With heavy steps, she found her way to a boardinghouse where the owner took pity on her and agreed to allow her to spend one night. A heavy heart dictated her dreams that night. Dreams where she found herself very much alone.

The next morning, sunlight peered through the window, making Adelaide feel a little better than the night before. She had given the matter to the Lord, and that's where it would stay. Quickly she got up and dressed. In order to find a stagecoach to return home, she'd have to hurry and make the arrangements. She'd grab a bite to eat first.

Once downstairs, she looked over to see a room full of men dining at the table. As hungry as she was, she didn't feel it proper to sit and eat with them, so she lifted her bag and walked through the door into the sunlight.

Walking only a few steps from the boardinghouse, she heard someone call her name. It almost sounded like Josiah's voice. She turned and looked in all directions. Nothing. Of course, she had imagined it. He seemed to follow her everywhere, even into her dreams.

Adelaide took a few more steps. The sound was clearer now, spoken directly behind her. She turned to see Josiah holding the hand of a beautiful little girl, the image of her father. Adelaide's heart melted.

When Adelaide glanced at Josiah, his questioning eyes held hers. For a moment, both seemed lost in words they couldn't speak. The look in Josiah's eyes warmed her clear through. She loved him. Oh, how she loved him.

Finally, Josiah's tender voice eased through the silence. "Grace, this is my wife, Adelaide. Adelaide, Grace."

"Hello, Grace," Adelaide said, scrunching down in front of the little girl. Grace lifted shy eyes to Adelaide. The little girl offered the faintest of smiles. Adelaide decided that was a good start.

"No question she belongs to you, Josiah." Adelaide chuckled.

He nodded with a grin. His expression grew serious. "We need to talk, Adelaide. Have you eaten breakfast?"

She shook her head.

"We saw you in the boardinghouse. We haven't eaten yet, either."

"You were there? You should eat there."

"No, I'd rather we have a little more privacy."

Together the three of them made their way to the restaurant. Adelaide wondered what the next hour would bring.

❧

Adelaide and Josiah spent most of their meal getting to know Grace. Little by little, the child talked, revealing snippets of her past to them. Already Adelaide could see herself mothering this child, with or without Josiah's love. They could be a family; she knew they could. If Josiah wanted them on the ship—though life would be hard on the sea—they'd somehow survive. Watching Elizabeth and Peter McCord with their daughter, Emma, had shown Adelaide that much.

"Will you be my mama?" Grace asked after she clumsily took a drink of water and wiped her mouth on her arm.

Adelaide stared into Josiah's eyes. Of course, he wanted her to say yes. He needed someone to look after Grace. Instead of the usual resentment, Adelaide had a sense of peace. "Yes, Grace, I will be your mama."

Grace took another bite of her egg, her pudgy legs swinging beneath her.

When Adelaide looked back at Josiah, what she saw on his face surprised her. She thought he would be happy to hear her say yes. Instead, he looked—how—sad? She couldn't put her finger on it, but something was definitely wrong.

Fears assailed her. Did he not even want her around anymore? The rejection caused her more pain than she cared to admit. Just when she thought she had things figured out, when it seemed all the answers were neatly in place, she found herself in a state of confusion once more.

"The beach is only a couple of blocks away. Can we talk there?" Josiah asked.

Adelaide nodded, fearing the worst.

ॐ

On the beach, Josiah found a couple of chairs for them. Grace immediately set to work building a sand castle while Josiah and Adelaide settled into their chairs. Josiah took off his cap and ran his fingers through his hair. Where would he begin? How could he tell Adelaide he was giving up the *Courage*? That his body would no longer allow him to do the rigorous work he once did. Would she think him an invalid? Why, he didn't even have a job.

Not only would she have to give up her dream of living on the sea, but she would be stuck with a man she didn't love. Further, she'd have a child to raise.

Nausea swelled in his stomach. No matter how he tried to word it in his mind, the truth still spelled misery to his future with Adelaide.

Grace busied herself a few feet away from them. Amazing how well children adapted to new situations. At least that was something for which he was thankful. Adelaide sat motionless in the chair beside him—no doubt waiting for him to spill what was on his mind.

He fingered the cap back and forth in his hands. "I guess you're wondering what I want to say?"

"Yes."

"I don't quite know how to tell you this, Adelaide." He could feel her looking at him. He looked down at his cap, searching for the words. Finally he turned to her. She looked so vulnerable. So beautiful. Oh, how he did not want to lose her! He cleared his throat and glanced back at his cap. "I know you love the sea, Adelaide. I would never take that away from you willingly."

He lifted his gaze in time to see confusion on her face. "If there was any other way, if I could do anything to make it work—"

Adelaide stretched out her hand and placed it on his arm. "Josiah, what is it?"

He fidgeted in his seat until he mustered the nerve to say the words. "I have to give up whaling." There. He'd said it. Fear would not let him look at her.

"But why? I could help you with Grace on the ship. We can do this."

He shook his head. "That's not it, Adelaide. I should have told you before, but I just couldn't bring myself to do it. Now, I have no choice. Remember when I struggled with the tropical fever?"

She nodded.

"I'm afraid the fever has taken its toll on me. I've not been the same since. When it left, it took my strength with it. Truth is, I'm too weak to do what it takes to captain a whaling ship." He swallowed back the pride, hating to admit he wasn't man enough to handle the workload. "I know you must hate me for what I've put you through, and now to take away your dream—"

"Josiah, I don't care about that."

"Well, it's just unthinkable that I would do that to you and—what?" He turned to her.

She smiled. "I said, I don't care about that."

"What do you mean?"

"I mean, I don't care if we can't sail."

Josiah looked at her with shocked disbelief. "But I thought—"

She laughed. "Well, I did, too. But the truth of the matter

is that Pa painted a much different picture than the life I found on the whaling ship. While I wouldn't trade the experience for anything and would be happy to continue whaling at your side, I'm equally happy, and more so, to live on land."

He couldn't believe his ears. She wanted to stay with him. More importantly, she actually sounded happy to stay with him. Before he could pull her into his arms, Grace came up to them.

"Look at my whaling ship," she said, pointing toward her rather awkward creation.

"Oh, Grace, it's absolutely beautiful." Adelaide reached over and, seeing the child did not back away, gave her a slight hug, to which Grace responded in kind.

"That's a mighty fine ship, Grace," Josiah agreed.

The child beamed at their praise.

"Grace, come here for a moment," Josiah said. She walked over to him. "Would you be terribly disappointed if we don't sail on a ship?"

Grace looked at him, puzzled.

"Adelaide and I, well, we want to find a real home on land with you right beside us. How would you like that?"

Grace smiled broadly, the first time they'd actually seen her pretty white teeth in a full, honest-to-goodness grin. "Can I play a little longer first?"

Josiah and Adelaide laughed. "Yes, indeed, you can," Josiah answered.

Grace skipped over to her creation.

"She's so much like you, Josiah."

He rubbed his chin. "She is, at that. Poor child."

Adelaide laughed. "Actually, I'm rather glad."

Josiah thought Adelaide looked as though she could kick herself for saying that. "I'm glad, too."

"You are?"

"Yes. If she had looked like Catherine, I would have had a daily reminder of my foolishness."

Adelaide looked at him. Josiah turned to her. "I never loved her, Adelaide. I see that now. Whatever I felt for Catherine pales in comparison to what I feel for you." Josiah tenderly covered her hands with his own. "I love you, and I want you to be my wife, in the truest sense of the word." Without a blink, his gaze held her breathless.

"Adelaide Sanborn Buchanan, will you marry me—again?"

twenty

Adelaide wondered if her heart would ever come back to her. It seemed to have taken wings and flown into paradise. "Oh, Josiah." She couldn't utter another word as the tears tumbled from her eyes.

"Is that a yes?" he asked with a laugh.

She continued to wipe away her tears and nodded vigorously. Before she could blink, Josiah jumped from his chair and scooped her into his arms.

He held her close, his face burrowed into her neck. His warm breath caused her skin to tingle. Lifting his head, he tenderly kissed her eyes, her nose, and finally her lips. Placing her on her feet, he pulled away slightly and looked at her. His fingers twirled a strand of hair that had escaped her bonnet. "You know, I'd still like to see your hair down sometime. I'll bet it's beautiful."

Adelaide's face burned as though someone held a candle only inches from her.

He smiled and kissed her once more, the emotion of recent days working its way through their kiss.

"I was going to stay in Bayview awhile for Grace to get acclimated to her new life, but she seems to be handling things just fine. I'll make arrangements for us to take the first stage back to Yorksville. I think there's one scheduled tomorrow. Then I'll look around for work."

Adelaide stepped back. "Oh, I almost forgot," she said suddenly, as if waking abruptly from a dream. "The Markles asked if we would consider taking over the general store. Their health is failing. They would retain part ownership, though most of it would go to us. They want to continue living in the upstairs apartment but said we could live downstairs and run the store."

Josiah stared at her wide-eyed. He shook his head. "I can't believe this."

"I hadn't given it much thought till now. I thought we would head back to the ship," she said.

"All my worrying, and God had everything taken care of from the start." He leaned his head back and stared at the sky. With a twist of his wrist, he threw his cap in the air and let out a long whoop. He grabbed Adelaide and twirled her around.

Grace giggled and ran toward them to join in the celebration. Josiah lowered Adelaide and the three of them joined hands and skipped in circles, laughing and praising the Lord together.

❧

Night breezes hovered over the sea, filling the air with a pleasant mist. Josiah finalized the arrangements, and together the little family headed back to the boardinghouse.

Grace skipped alongside Adelaide, holding her hand. "Can I call you Mama?" Grace seemed to have plucked the question from nowhere.

Adelaide turned to her with a start. She looked up to see Josiah staring at her. He threw her a wink. Adelaide turned back to Grace. "You certainly may call me Mama if you would like, dear."

Grace's pudgy hand squeezed Adelaide's. The little girl said nothing, but her walk turned into a happy trot. A nurturing instinct coursed through Adelaide. How she loved this child already!

Once they reached the boardinghouse, they climbed the stairs and stopped in front of Adelaide's room. She assumed they would get her things and move her into Josiah's room. Josiah turned to her. "I have made arrangements for you to stay in your room one more night, Adelaide."

A wave of disappointment swept over her. Did he notice?

"I want to marry you again. Really marry you. When we

get back to Yorksville, we will have a proper wedding. This time, you will truly become my wife."

Adelaide's cheeks burned. "Oh, Josiah, you don't need to do that."

He put his fingers to her lips. "I want to do this for you. For us." He lowered his head and placed a tender kiss upon her lips. Raising his opened hand to her, she put her key in his palm. With a tip of his head, he nodded toward her and opened the door, allowing her entrance. She turned and looked at him. Lifting the key, he pressed it into her palm. "I don't trust myself with it," he whispered with a wiggle of his eyebrows.

She laughed. Grace tugged at Adelaide's dress and snuggled next to her side. "Can I stay with you, Mama?"

Adelaide decided she liked the idea of being a mama. She looked at Josiah. If he was disappointed, he didn't show it. Most likely, he was a trifle nervous about dealing with a child, anyway. He nodded to her.

"Yes, of course, Grace, you may stay with me."

Her small face brightened.

Josiah winked. "Well, little family, I guess I'll see you in the morning."

"Good night, Josiah."

"Good night, Papa," Grace said as naturally as if she had known him all her life.

Josiah scrunched down and kissed Grace on the forehead. "Good night."

He stood. "Night, Addie."

Adelaide smiled, then closed the door, her heart beating wildly against her chest. She could hardly wait to go to bed and dream of the man she would soon marry—this time in every sense of the word.

❧

The trip to Yorksville passed by without a hitch. Once Adelaide introduced Grace to her family and they finished dinner, they settled in for a comfortable chat.

"So tell me about you two," Ma said while Esther skirted Grace out the door to check on the chickens.

Adelaide opened her mouth to speak, but Josiah raised his hand. "No, let me, Addie."

She stopped and nodded.

Ma looked at them curiously. For the next fifteen or so minutes, Josiah explained about the pretense of their wedding, the struggles along the way, the note about Grace, and finally where everything had brought them.

When he finished, Ma sat back in her chair and looked at them. "I knew something wasn't right. I just didn't know what." She looked at Adelaide. "I also knew that behind it all was something to do with your love for the sea."

Adelaide nodded, her eyes carefully avoiding Ma's.

Ma sat back up and brushed her hands together. "Well, that's that."

They both looked at her with a start. Adelaide felt sure they had a long talk coming to them.

Ma laughed. "What's to say?" She shrugged. "Everything's all right now, and that's what matters."

Relief rolled over Adelaide. "Thanks, Ma."

"I just want the two of you to be happy."

Adelaide reached for Josiah's hand and looked at him. "We are, Ma. We are." Josiah squeezed her hand.

Just then, Esther and Grace walked through the front door, holding hands. "Auntie Esther showed me the chickens." Grace ran over to Josiah. "She let me throw some feed on the floor, and they ran over to eat it. They make a funny sound. One almost bit me."

The words tumbled out of her faster than chicken feed from a bag. They all chuckled. Josiah looked at Adelaide. "She certainly seems to have overcome her shyness."

Adelaide agreed, muting a giggle behind her hand.

"Hey, I've got an idea," Josiah piped up. "How about after church tomorrow, we have a picnic at the beach?"

Grace clapped her hands together and jumped up and down, causing her loose bonnet to tilt in an awkward fashion on her head.

Once again they laughed. Everyone agreed the picnic would be a good idea. "We've also got a wedding to plan," Josiah said, his gaze never leaving Adelaide's.

❧

After church, old friends welcomed Adelaide and Josiah home with open arms. They'd had a good service, and now Adelaide looked forward to a picnic on the beach.

Ma fixed enough chicken to feed the church. They settled into place and ate a nice meal while Grace played in the sand.

"Esther, have you heard anything recently from Adam?" Josiah asked.

She shook her head, a pout on her lips.

Josiah laughed. "You'll hear soon, I'm sure. He's smitten with you, no doubt about that."

Her pout turned to a smile. "It's so hard not to have word." She fingered the gold chain around her neck.

"That's the tricky part of loving a seaman." He turned to Adelaide and grabbed her hand. "I'm glad we didn't have to go through that."

"Papa, come look," Grace shouted.

Josiah winked at Adelaide, and together they ran to Grace's side. They marveled at her sand creation and sang her praises. Josiah scooped her into his arms. Grace giggled and squealed as he twirled her round and round. When he finally placed her on the ground, she took crooked steps before finally falling into a heap. Grace turned to Josiah. "Again, Papa?"

Josiah groaned. "Oh, no, Grace. Papa's too dizzy."

"I'll race you back to the blanket, Grace," Adelaide called.

Josiah counted, "One, two, three." They took off trudging through the sinking sand, leaving Grace behind with her pudgy legs to carry her. It suddenly became a real race for Josiah and Adelaide, though her skirts got in the way. By the time they reached the blanket, they fell together, laughing and gasping for breath. Adelaide looked at his blue eyes as he smiled only inches from her, wanting desperately to kiss him but not with her family around. She quickly straightened herself.

"Good to hear you so happy, Adelaide," Ma said.

"I am happy, Ma."

"I talked to the pastor this morning. The wedding is set for tomorrow," Josiah said.

"So soon?" Ma asked.

"Why wait? We're not inviting lots of people, just family, the Markles, a couple of witnesses, and, well. . .um. . .why wait?"

They all let out a laugh. Adelaide's emotions rose to her face. She wished she weren't so transparent.

❧

A pleasant evening breeze caused a strand of hair to tickle Adelaide's cheek as she made her way to the church. She felt glad they had decided on a church wedding. They wanted a different start this time.

Adelaide lifted her dress—the dress Josiah had bought her on the island—so that she could more easily climb the church steps. She adjusted the wreath of flowers that circled her head.

Having the matter of the store settled with the Markles made her feel a lot better. She and Josiah had already taken their things to the store and would move in after the wedding. The Markles left some furniture for them since Josiah and Adelaide hadn't had time to set up housekeeping as of yet. Grace seemed all too happy to stay with Ma and Esther for a couple of days.

Adelaide wondered if she had stepped into a fairy tale. She couldn't believe how their story had changed for the better. With a thankful heart, she entered the church. Josiah stood with his back to her, talking with Pastor Daugherty. Pastor looked up and Josiah turned. The pleasure on his face made Adelaide's heart skip. She made her way toward him. He stepped forward and grabbed her hand. "You look beautiful." His breath tickled her ear as he whispered the words meant for her alone.

The pastor began the wedding service, and Adelaide's heart soared. Surrounded by family and friends, standing by the man she loved with all her heart, and with a precious little girl whom they would raise together, Adelaide whispered a prayer of thanks deep in her soul.

When the ceremony ended, Josiah reached over and kissed his wife. Though he didn't make a spectacle, this kiss was different from all the others. A kiss that said they belonged to one another, and nothing would ever change that.

The little group went to Ma's house, ate a wonderful meal together, laughed, and shared stories. Finally, one by one, they trickled away, each going to their own homes.

"Mrs. Buchanan, are you ready to go home?"

Adelaide looked up to see Josiah's blue eyes sparkling down at her, his extended hand ready to help her to her feet.

She smiled, the thrill of truly being his wife running through her. They said their good-byes and headed for the Markles' General Store. Their new home.

The *clip-clop* of horses' hooves echoed through the night sky. The sea murmured softly in the distance. Adelaide leaned into Josiah. He held her tightly with one arm and guided the horses with the other. She thought the night perfect.

"Do you miss the sea, Josiah?"

"I will always miss it some. It's been a part of my life for as long as I can remember. But I have everything I want with you and Grace." He turned to her. "I couldn't be happier." He kissed her long and hard. The team almost ran off the path. They laughed while Josiah snapped the reins to speed the horses along.

Josiah put the carriage away, and Adelaide noticed the lights were out upstairs, so the Markles had already gone to bed. She climbed the steps to the porch and waited as Josiah had requested. He soon joined her and stopped in front of her. "I've never done this before," he said as he lifted her into his arms. Adelaide giggled. Josiah nuzzled his nose into her neck. "But then I've never been in love like this before."

Adelaide shivered slightly. Josiah carried her through the doorway, then pushed open the door to the bedroom, Adelaide still in his arms. He lowered her to the floor. "I would like to offer our marriage to the Lord."

Adelaide nodded.

Together they knelt beside their bed.

"Father, we thank Thee for bringing us to this place. Thank Thee for providing us with an income through the Markles' generosity. Adelaide's right. Life is all about choices. Our choices affect not only ourselves but others around us. I thank Thee for helping me make the right choices this time. Thank Thee for bringing Adelaide into my life. And while I hadn't planned on Grace, Thou didst know all about her, and I thank Thee for bringing her into our lives. May our family bring Thee the honor Thou dost deserve. May we be an extension of Thy love, grace, and mercy. And one day may we gather as a circle unbroken before Thy throne where we will hear Thee say, 'Well done, thou good and faithful servant. . . .'

"Now, Father, I pray Thy blessings on our family as we begin our lives together. In Jesus' name, amen."

Adelaide whispered, "Amen."

They rose and stepped away from the bed. Josiah went and closed the bedroom door. He walked back toward Adelaide and looked her square in the face. "I will spend my life proving my love for you."

"And I, you, Josiah. I love you." She brushed the tears that pooled in her eyes and stretched her arms around his neck. He pulled her close to him and kissed her in the way of which she had always dreamed.

When they parted, Josiah looked at her. "You know, whaling has been good to me. Provided a substantial living, true, but most of all it brought me you." Josiah grew silent and serious as his fingers reached for her hair. Slowly, tenderly, his hands pulled away tiny pins, one by one. Adelaide barely breathed. Josiah's fingers caressed the honey brown curls that fell in heaps across her shoulders. He leaned into her, his voice brushing light against her ear as his hands continued to explore her hair. "I told you I'd like it down," he said in a heavy whisper.

Everything around Adelaide seemed surreal. Was it really happening? If she breathed, would the magic end? She wanted to stay in the moment forever.

Holding onto her hand, Josiah took three steps, stopped at the stand beside their bed, and in one puff of air, blew out their candle.

Into the darkness he whispered, "I choose you, Adelaide Buchanan. I choose you."

A Letter To Our Readers

Dear Reader:

In order that we might better contribute to your reading enjoyment, we would appreciate your taking a few minutes to respond to the following questions. We welcome your comments and read each form and letter we receive. When completed, please return to the following:

Fiction Editor
Heartsong Presents
PO Box 719
Uhrichsville, Ohio 44683

1. Did you enjoy reading *A Whale of a Marriage* by Diann Hunt?
   ❏ Very much! I would like to see more books by this author!
   ❏ Moderately. I would have enjoyed it more if

   _____

   _____

   _____

2. Are you a member of **Heartsong Presents**?   ❏ Yes   ❏ No
   If no, where did you purchase this book? _____

   _____

3. How would you rate, on a scale from 1 (poor) to 5 (superior), the cover design? _____

4. On a scale from 1 (poor) to 10 (superior), please rate the following elements.

   ____ Heroine   ____ Plot
   ____ Hero   ____ Inspirational theme
   ____ Setting   ____ Secondary characters

5. These characters were special because?_____

_____

_____

6. How has this book inspired your life?_____

_____

_____

7. What settings would you like to see covered in future
   Heartsong Presents books? _____

_____

_____

8. What are some inspirational themes you would like to see
   treated in future books? _____

_____

_____

9. Would you be interested in reading other **Heartsong
   Presents** titles? ❏ Yes ❏ No

10. Please check your age range:
    ❏ Under 18   ❏ 18-24
    ❏ 25-34   ❏ 35-45
    ❏ 46-55   ❏ Over 55

Name_____

Occupation _____

Address _____

City_____ State_____ Zip_____

Chesapeake

4 stories in 1

$\mathcal{T}$he Chesapeake region of the mid-nineteenth century holds days tested by sorrow and renewed by hope. Meet four couples about to be faced with their greatest challenges—can they also find their greatest joys?

Author Loree Lough has woven four faith-filled tales of romance that are sure to bring heartwarming satisfaction.

Contemporary, paperback, 464 pages, 5 $^3/_{16}$"x 8"

Heartsong

Presents

HEARTSONG ❤ PRESENTS

Love Stories Are Rated G!

That's for godly, gratifying, and of course, great! If you love a thrilling love story but don't appreciate the sordidness of some popular paperback romances, **Heartsong Presents** is for you. In fact, **Heartsong Presents** is the premiere inspirational romance book club featuring love stories where Christian faith is the primary ingredient in a marriage relationship.

Sign up today to receive your first set of four, never-before-published Christian romances. Send no money now; you will receive a bill with the first shipment. You may cancel at any time without obligation, and if you aren't completely satisfied with any selection, you may return the books for an immediate refund!

Imagine. . .four new romances every four weeks—two historical, two contemporary—with men and women like you who long to meet the one God has chosen as the love of their lives. . .all for the low price of $10.99 postpaid.

To join, simply complete the coupon below and mail to the address provided. **Heartsong Presents** romances are rated G for another reason: They'll arrive Godspeed!

YES! Sign me up for Heartsong!